Advance p

Boatman grabs you by throat and drags you kicking and screaming through his prose. With a dash of Lansdale and a smattering of Martin's Wild Cards, the tales within inhabit the dark and nasty side of our souls; and throughout Boatman infuses it all with a keen wit and an eye for detail. And when he lets you up to breathe, like God, you might just find yourself laughing. This is the sort of stuff I like to read as the bells sound midnight.

Paul Haines award-winning author of **Doorways for the Dispossessed**

Boatman's debut collection will knock you down and kick you in the teeth. Alternately hysterical, grotesque, bizarre, and fantastic, Boatman's collection is a must-read for anyone itching to get their hands on fresh new fiction that pulls no punches.

Ronald Damien Malfi, author of **The Nature of Monsters** and **The Fall of Never**

I was once a young horror fan who became an old small press writer and then a publisher. I like to think I may have discovered and helped a few good genre writers get their stuff into print over the years. Michael Boatman was a name I knew from television and the movies, but I must admit, I found myself most blown away by his potential as a writer. This collection certainly validates my initial impressions, and now you should reward yourself by reading these wonderful gems of prose.

Bob Gunner
CEO and Publisher Fat Cat New Media Inc./Cyber-Pulp Press

Michael Boatman writes like a visitor from hell. Someone out on short term leave for bad behavior. I love this stuff. He's one of the new, and more than promising, writers making his mark, and a dark and wonderful mark it is.

Joe R. Lansdale

Michael Boatman
4-27-08

God Laughs When You Die
Mean Little Stories from the Wrong Side of the Tracks

Michael Boatman

Dybbuk Press
October 2007, New York, NY
http://www.dybbuk-press.com

Publishing History
Folds © Michael Boatman 2007
The Tarantula Memoirs © Michael Boatman 2006, originally appeared in SUPERHEROFICTION.com in 2003
The Drop © Michael Boatman 2004, originally appeared in Horror Garage, issue 3 by Under the Volcano, Inc.
Katchina © Michael Boatman 2005. First appeared in Revenant. A Horror Anthology. Carnifex Press
Bloodbath at Landsdale Towers © Michael Boatman 2006, Originally appeared in Badass Horror by Dybbuk Press
Dormant © Michael Boatman 2007, originally appeared in Lightning, by Under the Volcano, Inc.
The Ugly Truth © Michael Boatman 2005. Originally appeared in Sages & Swords. Pitch Black Books
The Long Lost Life of Bleak © Michael Boatman 2007
The Last American President © Michael Boatman 2006. First appeared in Red Scream, issue 0.2 2005

Introduction © David J. Schow 2007

All Illustrations copyrighted by their illustrators as cited on page 8.

ISBN: 0-9766546-2-8
Long ISBN: 978-09766546-2-9
Library of Congress Control Number: 2007920114

Printed in the United States of America
Cover adapted from "The Cure of Folly"
by Hieronymus Bosch

To Myrna, who tolerates my strangeness.
And to Jordan, MacKenzie, Aidan and Jacob - the four points of the compass that guides my heart.

Table of Contents

Illustrations

Mike Laughs When You Read
By David J. Schow

Most of you think you know this man Boatman.

You watch movies, TV shows, and you can Google. You've formed opinions predicated on celebrity, performance, publicity, dish, or hearsay; and you think you know what you're talking about. Right about now you may be experiencing the sensation that maybe; just maybe you've missed the boat, man.

I had no idea that Michael Boatman had been keeping tabs on me; forming similar logic chains. He's sneaky like that. I had even less of a shred of an idea that Mike actually possessed a slant of mind and tilted POV very akin to my own forms of functional dementia. And I had even less than a biopsy of a molecule of a notion that Mike had been driven by the friendly demons inside his skull to write some of this stuff down - as stories.

Not a clue had I. Who knew?

When I mentioned "tilted POV," above, you need merely recall the visual significators found in any old Twilight Zone episode (one of the good ones), where our narrative is rolling nicely along, and suddenly we're hit with what cameramen call a "Dutch angle," which means that what we're seeing suddenly veers off-axis, the frame skews from a square to a parallelogram, and the borders of the boxed picture seem to melt and run, distorting what is seen (usually with the help of a good 18-mil lens to impart a fisheye effect with which you may also be familiar). It's one of the simplest tricks in the repertoire of the cinematographer, but one of the most effective.

Abruptly your reliance on the fidelity of your narrator has been cast into doubt; your "I-guy" has become a trickster. You are aware that the window through which you are witnessing the fictive reality of a photoplay may be imposing its own alien bias on the story. This is a very potent form of magic, not to be wielded by amateurs. Every storyteller depends on a tacit pact between performer and audience: You sit still and I'll tell you a story. Go a little further, trust me, suspend your disbelief and buy into my "what-if," and I just might tell you a real asskicker of a story.

Mike sent me some stories and it quickly became clear that he had jumped right to the asskicking part, smash cut.

Now obviously this writer/reader compact will not work for people who dully absorb their fiction with that old I-just-want-to-be-entertained attitude. That's great if you prefer to sit and sponge up words or images that do nothing but kill your time. But if you like to be goosed, thrilled and enlightened, you are risking the ultra-keen edge of participation, and that's much more fun. That's the difference between a run-of-the-mill horror story and what the Germans have seen fit to call phantastiche literatur.

Horror stories are presumed to be these neat little envelopes of dread to be opened and shut at will, not letter bombs that detonate in your face and spray you with the harsh reality of your own reliably ingrained phobias about sex, race, or ideologies. Bang — you're not looking out of safe window at a disposable fear; you're looking in a goddamned mirror, and you may deny what you see, but there it is ... then Boatman tilts the friggin' mirror and the world goes all funhouse on you. That's the phantastiche - chimerical, grotesque, fanciful, wild, magnificent in its exuberance.

Lesser horror stories are content to bitch slap the reader with a gross-out, but our own Mr. Boatman arrives with an innate understanding that gross-outs are not only entry level, but - hell - they're kind of funny in their extremes. The worst ones are usually just an overload of forensic detail. The best ones make you laugh and recoil at the same time. For this, one needs Michael's knack for the apocalyptic simile ("The mattress smelled like the septic field of a Mexican abortion clinic at high tide") or the one-step-beyond metaphor ("the kind of chemical satisfaction that squirmed its way down into your DNA, checked out the accommodations and said 'Make Room for Daddy'").

Also, he uses the word "normalcy" correctly. Not "normality." I appreciate that. Plus, he sold many of these tales piecemeal to places that would publish them - ink on paper, so you're not reading some wannabe's internet delusions of talent or blogsturbation - until they piled up and demanded a book with a suitably provocative title as their more permanent home.

Which brought me to the concept of BAM. Once Michael and I compared notes it became rapidly obvious that one of us was the other's Brudder from Anudder Mudda.

The ingredients of his youthful corruption cocktail were much as one might suspect: Monster mags, post-EC comics, Twilight Zone reruns and Night Gallery first-runs; those 1950s creature features with the best titles ever (think Attack of the Giant Leeches); Tolkien, Bradbury; read The Exorcist at age seven and somehow saw Night of the Living Dead before he was into double digits ... and yes, splatterpunk galvanized him like a hot shot of adrenalin straight into the heartmeat.

Nevertheless, you are probably visualizing Michael as that nice, personable light-comedy guy. And yet, like many horror writers denied the opportunity to craft good comedy (even though the tension-release architecture of funny stuff and scary stuff is distinctly parallel) Mike the horror enthusiast never got to crowbar Mike the actor-guy into anything remotely horrific. (Well, he finally made it - as I write this - into a theatrical production of Noel Coward's *Blithe Spirit,* and that at least allows him to rub shoulders with a ghost, but you perceive my point.)

So he put his rage on the page.

Michael suggests the disenfranchised among us - the street dregs, the burnouts, the washups, the dimly-glimpsed otherworld of discards and those supposedly beneath our civilized notice - have powers we cannot suspect, because once we recognize the power, it's already too late for us to report. Further, a higher social caste will not necessarily armor you; witness "Folds."

Good horror intrudes. It butts into your nice, safe sinecure and rustles up trouble. Sometimes it drips green on your carpet or molests your dog. Sometimes it shakes your perceptions like a terrier with a rat. Sometimes, the intrusion can change ... everything, from the way you deadbolt your doors to the way you get your own POV slanted anew. Read for entertainment if you wish. Or read with a tilted eye toward learning new ways of staying aware, vigilant against night terrors that don't wait until dark to get all up in your shit.

Among your guides are a potent bouillabaisse of characters like Mohammed "Chun King"

Jefferson, Stanky Methuselah, the Reverend Rufus Bleak, the Night Mother, Molo Pigsplitter, Jack Greer (aka The Tarantula), Death (him, her, or itself), the President, and the Black Possum. (I am saddened that you do not yet get to meet Harmony Tremontane and O-gazm of "The Gravity of Her Gaze," or Ms. Wrong-Number-Who-Gives-a-Fuck of "Our Kind of People," but maybe they'll make it into a future collection.)

You'll go uptown to TV studios and downmarket to the ends of the earth, with a whiff of science fiction (if not futurism) here and there like a kick of imported spice. Quiet shivers, repellent revelations and a summer blockbuster of splatter or two await you. Zombie fans may be encountering the word zuvembie here for the first time (I used it in a story a long time ago and an idiot editor changed it; likewise the even more obscure zombi).

I appreciate that Michael knows that word too.

If night is something more for you than the coming of darkness, if you would like to visit "a place where the dead dance in fields of blood-red violets; where the air is black with power and the earth is seeded with ashes," then let Michael take you for a little ride.

And you thought you knew this man Boatman.

13

FOLDS

He was five years old and he was fat.

Not the kind of "baby fat" that haunts the cheek and jowls of the average chubby American kid. Mohammed "Chun King" Jefferson weighed nearly a hundred twenty pounds *after* we'd stripped him down to his adult diaper.

And this was before he started in on the smorgasbord we'd offloaded onto THE MORRIE STAPLER SHOW stage.

"I don't understand it, Morrie," the mother, a pretty young thing of Chinese-American ancestry, said. "He wasn't always like this. When he was born he was..."

The mother stopped herself in mid-sentence and glanced over at her hog-sized chunk of offspring. Chun King was eating his way through enough junk food to poison a busload of Russian shot putters. He never even looked up.

"Jesus," I breathed. "Jerry, pull back and get me a low wide shot of the kid and the food. Then go in fast."

Jerry Salazar, the operator on Camera Two swooped in on the junior behemoth from the right side of the studio. I swore as the image of Chun King Jefferson, messy of mouth and surrounded by mountains of processed carbohydrates, swelled to cinematic proportions.

The studio audience loved it.

As the Co-Executive Producer and Director for MORRIE, I'd signed off on booking the mother/son act. I'd made all the customary promises, referrals for counselors plus a videotaped copy of the show to play for their hillbilly relatives.

It was all standard bullshit, stated simply and without multi-syllables, to get everybody snuggly with the fact that we were asking these people to degrade themselves before a rabid national audience. I even shook hands with the mother before she signed the waivers.

Now, as the studio filled with "ooohs" and "aaahs," I patted myself on the bank account.

"Don't you move, Jerry," I hissed over the headsets.

"I mean, he's normal in other ways, Morrie," the mother said. "It's just...you know..."

"You're worried about your child, dammit," Morrie said.

"Uh oh," Cray Donavan, my associate producer, mumbled.

"S.M.3."

I nodded. "Somebody ate his Prune Puffs this morning."

Morrie Stapler had three "Sympathetic Modes" for when he wanted to torque the studio audience. S.M. 3 was the one he used when he wanted to appear understanding while maintaining his trademark no nonsense image. Morrie's *I feel your pain, but I'm also fairly sure you're responsible for it* brand of tough love had knocked 'em for a loop back in Morristown New Jersey, where he served as the Honorable *Mayor* Morrie for two infamous terms, before taking the national airwaves by storm.

I hated Morrie Stapler. But, God help me, I loved my job.

"Of course we all *understand* that, Sue," Morrie said.

"But I'm concerned about little Mohammed. Didn't it ever occur to you to take him to a doctor?"

"I've taken him to so many doctors," the mother said. "None of them can figure out what's wrong with him."

"He eats too damn much," one audience member quipped.

The audience went nuts.

"Camera Three! Pull in. Pull in. Pull in!"

As the mother's face loomed large on monitor 3, I watched her eyes. She held her chin high while she waited for the laughter and the shouting to die down. She glared out over the audience, her eyes focused on some point far away from my studio.

The Fading Queen, I thought.

It was an old habit of mine, a holdover from the days when I wrote stories instead of copy; find some remarkable trait in a person and bequeath them a romantic title to match. Susan Jefferson seemed to shine with the quiet dignity of a Queen. Believe me; that quality set her apart from the scandal-hungry dunderheads that usually fill out our Friday afternoon audiences.

"I believe her," I said.

Cray Donavan cocked his head at me. "What did you say?" he said.

"I think she's really looking for help," I said.

"Yeah, right. Help," Donavan said, staring into the glowing electronic abyss. Onstage, Chun King was upending a family sized bag of Extra Cheezy GORDITOS into his yawning soup bucket.

"These idiots sell every scrap of human dignity for a few minutes on TV," Donovan said. "Just so they can be slobbered over like mini-celebrities when they get back to whatever hellish burg spawned them."

17

"I know," I said, the sound of my own philosophy banging in my ears. "But something about this one..."

Donavan was staring at me with the kind of suspicion I typically reserve for 'reformed' sexual predators.

"Forget it," I said.

Donavan shrugged and went back to studying the monitor.

But I was growing more and more unsettled by the emotion flickering in Susan Jefferson's eyes. I was ill-equipped to cope with sincerity at that particular plateau in my career. To say that I'd become jaded would be putting it mildly.

"Camera Four, give me a quick pass over the audience," I said. Toni Rinaldi, the operator on 4, panned her crane-mounted camera over the audience as ordered.

"Right there," I said. "B.B.W. on 3 looks good to go."

The image on monitor 4 changed as 3 pulled back and Rinaldi swooped down to snatch a tight closeup of the tears on the B.B.W.'s face.

"That's alright, girlfriend," shrieked the Big Black Woman when she realized a camera was looking in her direction. "You a good mother!"

"Yeah," I said, breathing easier.

"Much better."

***

"Am I the only one who's hearing this shit?"

Sarah Chang, my line producer, glared at Morrie with an expression that would have turned him to stone if he were human.

"I'm talking about John and Jane Q Public, Sarah," Morrie said. "Way out in the cornfields and ghettos of Asshole America. In Asshole America, things are a little more "black and white," if you catch my drift."

"Morrie, that's..."

"Blacks, white trash, maybe a few Hispanics thrown in for variety, Sarah. That's who Asshole America wants to see in their living rooms. Look at our audience polls: *Asian doesn't fly in syndication.*"

"Morrie..." Chang said, white-knuckling her pen.

"Christ, Sarah, I thought I'd stumbled into one of those goofy Jackie Chan pictures, only no funny black guy and no chop-chop!"

Chang threw her pad down and stood up.

I was dying to get out of there. All I could think of was the damaged nobility I'd seen in Susan Jefferson's eyes.

And Morrie was making a complete jackass of himself.

"Morrie, that's the biggest load of corporate media racist bullshit I've ever heard," Chang said.

"What the hell's wrong with you?" Morrie said.

Chang removed her glasses and shoved them into the pocket of her denim shirt.

"You, Morrie," Chang snapped. "You're a racist."

"I am not a racist!"

"Morrie, in case you hadn't noticed, I'm Asian. You can't make racially chauvinistic statements like that *when I'm in the fucking room!* You're a Jew, for God's sake. I'd expect you to know better."

"Hey! Now hold on here, Sarah."

19

"What have you got against Asians then, Morrie?"

"Oh please, girlfriend," Morrie snorted. "You're from Pomona, for God's sake. You're as Asian as I am."

"Jesus, Morrie!"

"Look at Marcus: He's black and you don't see him complaining."

Chang looked over at me.

"Yes, Marcus," she said. "How do you put up with Morrie's racist bullshit?"

Chang and I had spent many late nights fantasizing about ways to kill Morrie off the show, but when you have a winning horse you don't jump off mid-race. Not if you want to stay afloat in television.

I repeated that to myself as I recalled the previous week's ratings: Top Ten with all the right demographics. That meant a big Christmas bonus for me, plus a decent piece of the syndication pie.

"Son-of-a-bitch," Chang sighed. "Try not to drool on the carpet, Marcus."

***

You never forget the sound a fist makes when it strikes flesh. My father used his fists on my sister and me for years before he died of heart failure one Christmas Eve. The following Christmas morning was the happiest either one of us could remember in a long time.

But you never forget the sound.

I heard it as I was walking back to my car after the show: bone wrapped in meat punishing softer meat, followed by the muffled whimper and the dull thud of a head striking concrete.

Something in that cry held me rooted to the spot. The meat sound repeated, and this time the cry of pain was loud enough for me to locate its source. It was coming from behind a busted down Nissan idling a few feet to my left.

Leaning down, I could see two figures struggling on the concrete. I heard the terrible sound again, and before I knew what I was doing, I had run around to the other side of the Nissan.

The attacker knelt above the woman's chest, pinning her to the ground beneath his bulk. As I watched he lifted a heavy arm and struck her across the face.

I was so stunned that I couldn't move.

But my mouth still worked.

"Hey!" I shouted.

The attacker looked up, mid-blow, and the world lurched beneath my feet. It was Chun King Jefferson.

The fat toddler was sitting, not kneeling as I had thought before; he was sitting on his mother's chest.

As I watched, Chun King turned, wrapped his hands around his mother's throat and banged her head against the concrete, hard.

I grabbed him by the collar and hauled him off of her, revulsion making me rougher than I intended. I flung him away from her with such force that he hit the ground with a loud thud. He started to cry, a loud, squawking bark, more roar than whimper.

"Don't hurt him!" the mother cried.

And for a fleeting instant, I was sure she was speaking to Chun King, not to me.

"He...he was attacking you," I stammered stupidly. Then I knelt to help her up.

21

Susan Jefferson sat with her back against the passenger side front door of the little Nissan. She held her head in her hands and began to cry.

"Are you alright?" I asked.

"You think I'm stupid, like the rest of them," she said.

"Jesus," I said. "What the hell's going on here?"

"I'm not stupid," she whispered. "I'm not like the other people on your show. Neither is Mohammed."

She got to her feet and retrieved her wailing five-year old. He'd gone limp, allowing her to pick him up as if he hadn't just tried to fracture her skull. Remarkably, she was able to heft him into the back seat of their car. He was too big to fit into a standard car seat.

"Listen," I said. "I don't know what..."

"We need help," she interrupted. "I can't control what he eats anymore."

She said this last so quietly that I almost missed it. Once again I was struck by the quality of desperation that shone from her.

It's called honesty, asshole, I thought. *You remember that, don't you?*

"You promised us some help," she said. "I'm at the end of my rope."

The flutter in my stomach that began when I saw her on the monitors kicked up a notch.

"Have you tried family counseling?" I volunteered.

It's the standard line used by all producers when confronted by a distraught guest. This time, however, I meant it. After what I'd just seen I would have made the calls myself. "I can refer you to someone..."

"We've done that," she said. "We've been to so many therapists, so many clinics..." She paused, as if searching for the correct words. Then she looked me in the eye and said, "He won't stop eating."

Her eyes returned to the cement between her feet.

"And there are other things..."

She was interrupted by a wail from inside the car. Her eyes widened; then squeezed shut.

"Are you okay?" I asked.

The windows of her car were all closed, but I could see Chun King sitting inside, staring out at us. His mouth was hinged open like a trapdoor, that high-pitched whine cycling up and out of him like the shriek of an air raid siren.

"He's hungry," the mother said.

"What?" I asked, disbelieving. "He can't be hungry. Not after all the..."

I was about to say, *Not after all the garbage we let him hammer down his throat.*

"I have to go," the mother whispered. "If I don't get him something he'll get upset."

"Wait a minute," I said.

If she heard me she gave no sign. Susan Jefferson turned and bolted for her car.

"Hey! Wait!" I yelled. "Mrs. Jefferson!"

As she reached for the driver's door, the mother stumbled. I caught her just as her knees buckled. During the taping, I noticed that she was thin. We'd joked about it in the booth, *Skinny Mom Says: Help! My Child is Obese!!!* We'd seen it a million times on the MORRIE show.

But as my hands brushed the sides of her ribcage, I felt the jut of bone beneath her blouse. She felt as fragile as porcelain, as flimsy as a child's doll cobbled together from dried twigs. I gasped, animal reflex robbing me of social graces for a moment.

I could hear the kid screaming.

"I'm sorry," Susan whispered.

I heard the grief in her voice, and the sheer exhaustion, as she threw open the door and flung herself into the car. I bent down and looked into the car. Chun King screamed louder. From where I stood his open mouth looked enormous, his features contorted in a grimace of need and...

Hate

The scream went on and on, seemingly without benefit of breath. He turned toward me, and when he did, his expression...changed. He lunged across the seat and smashed his fist into the window, inches from my face.

I fell backward and landed flat on my ass amid the tinkling chime of broken glass. The scream of burning rubber momentarily drowned out the boy's shrieks as the Nissan screeched away. I could only stare as the little car slammed over a speed bump, slewed onto the street and shot away into the darkness.

I sat there, immobilized by the memory of the boy's eyes, the unmistakable message they bore just before he smashed the window. *Stay away from us. Don't interfere.*

I'm in control.

It took me a moment to convince my lungs to contract but I finally won the argument. As that first breath hitched in my chest, I put my face in my hands and wept.

I believe I knew, even then, that Chun King Jefferson was going to be the death of me.

The next morning, I broke two cardinal rules: I drove into my office on Saturday, sifted through the contact list for the last show, and located the Jeffersons' phone number.

I told myself that I was being ridiculous. This was a five year old boy after all. How much damage could he be capable of?

There are...other things.

I ignored the gooseflesh marching up and down my arms and dialed the number, unable to forget Susan Jefferson's eyes, her apparent inability to save herself.

Save herself from what? I thought.

"Hello?"

It was a kid's voice.

It's Chun King and he's going to kill you.

"Is...is your mommy there?" I said, hating the fear in my own voice.

"I can't talk to you," the kid on the other end of the connection said. "I'll get in trouble."

"Can I talk to your mommy?" I said. "It's very important that I speak with her."

"She's gone."

Something cold unfurled itself in the pit of my stomach.

"I'll get in trouble," the kid repeated listlessly.

There was something about the kid's voice, a buzzing asexual monotone that set my teeth on edge.

"I have to go now."

The line went dead.

I sat at my desk for a long time, staring at the contact list. I had the Jeffersons' address. I could have just driven out there.

"Tell 'em they've won an all expenses paid trip to Hawaii courtesy of the Morrie Stapler Show," I said to no one in particular. "1st Place for America's Most Fucked Up Family!""

Any excuse would have been sufficient.

"You need a vacation, pal," I said finally.

I crumpled up the contact sheet and tossed it into the trash bin. Then I stood up, walked to my door and turned out the lights.

"Too much time in the fucking freak show."

I went home.

***

"She claims that she spoke with you a few weeks ago," my assistant Gina, said. "Something about her son's condition?"

Gina handed me the note and walked out of the director's booth. I'd spent the weeks since the incident in the parking lot trying not to think about Susan Jefferson. As time and toil pulled me further away from that strange episode, a welcome sense of normalcy had crept back into my life.

But I couldn't sleep.

I'd tried pills, prescription and otherwise, booze, sometimes all three simultaneously. Whenever I neared the edges of sleep, however, the memory of her eyes barred my way. I became adept at faking my way through the days. No one knew I was falling apart.

The show that day was called "UFO PROSTITUTES! ARE YOU A HO' FOR E.T?" We were on a commercial break while the security guards broke up a fight between a woman who claimed to be "a willing sexual recruiter for the "Venusians who secretly rule the Earth" and a teenaged girl who claimed she'd contracted "Space Herpes" from her alien boyfriend, a stand-up individual with a spotty mustache named "Prince Remulex."

While the combatants were led off the set, I read the note.

Please help us. You promised.

***

I found the small house easily enough.

It sat on a nondescript street near a decommissioned Air Force base, two hours east of LA. The house was in terrible disrepair. Two cars sat up on cinderblocks in the barren front yard.

The front door was wide open.

A child stood in the darkened entry hall, just beyond the open door. A single bare light bulb burned over the child's head. In the ugly yellow light I could make out the same black curly hair I remembered, the same wide, up-tilted eyes and full lips.

Help me. He won't stop eating.

But it wasn't Chun King. It was a girl, taller, older by three or four years and thinner by thirty or forty pounds. Black bruises encircled her eyes. Her lips and chin were stained with something that looked like dried blood.

"My mommy's sick," the little girl said.

She stepped back, out of the light. I stepped over the threshold and out of the dry desert wind. The girl closed the door behind me.

The first thing I noticed was the heat.

It was too warm inside the little house. Tepid pulses of stale air gusted over me where I stood in the center of the hall. Despite the fact that it was at least eighty degrees outside, someone had turned up the thermostat.

The house was a mess. Empty fast food cartons lay all over the floor. The sofa and lounge chair in the corner were covered with open containers of half-eaten TV dinners and empty potato chip bags.

"Where's your mommy?" I said.

"My mommy's sick."

The girl's eyes shone as she looked up at me. She was nearly as thin as the woman I'd met in the parking lot. Her light brown complexion had gone the sallow color of moldy cheese. Her skin glistened with a sheen of sweat that plastered her thin black hair across her skull.

She turned and walked into the guts of the house.

I set my briefcase down on the floor and followed her into the kitchen. I wiped my sleeve along my forehead, trying to stop droplets of sweat from running down into my eyes. Moving through the house was like walking through a dry sauna.

Pots and pans covered with old food sat piled in the sink. An odor like rotten milk and ancient cat litter hung, so thick it was almost visible, in the warm air.

"She said you would come," the girl said, as she led me into the rear of the house toward one of the back bedrooms. "She said you would keep your promise."

"What's happened?" I asked. "Does your mommy need a doctor? What's wrong?"

But as we turned the corner into the master bedroom, I saw what was wrong inside that house.

Susan Jefferson was lying in bed, half propped up against the headboard. Her face was drawn, her cheeks hollowed out from deprivation. Her dull brown eyes stared out from deep black sockets.

Everyone has seen the Sad Children, the ones in faraway places like Ethiopia, El Salvador or the Philippines - the children who lie dying in their own filth, too exhausted to brush away the flies that crawl across their too-wide eyes. *That's* what she looked like, lying there on a filthy mattress in a two bedroom house on the edge of the Mojave Desert.

That room felt like the inside of a sweat lodge, but she was too dehydrated to sweat. A filthy sheet half-covered her, her naked shoulders jutting like jagged coral reefs from beneath. One of her legs hung over the side of the bed, a broomstick with a small foot attached at the end - the toenails too long - more like claws.

"Oh my God," I said into the alien atmosphere of the small bedroom.

I took a step backward and something crunched beneath my foot. I looked down to see that I was standing in a half empty box of ENGLEMAN'S FAT FREE POWDERED DONUTS.

"What's wrong with her?" I stammered.

"He takes," the pale little girl whispered. "He takes."

That's when I realized that something was moving under the sheet.

I thought it was a pile of dirty clothes: mounds of discarded clothing lay everywhere. Every open surface in the room was covered with half-eaten food and trash. I could smell the sour tang of stale nacho chips and rotten milk beneath the odor of sweat.

Whatever was under the sheet moved again.

"What the hell is that?" I said.

29

The girl remained silent as she walked around to the side of the bed and stood at her mother's side. Susan Jefferson reached up and hooked her fingers into the front of the t-shirt the girl wore.

The girl's eyes never left mine as she reached down and removed the limp hand from her shoulder. Then she pulled back the sheet and showed me what was under it.

I stood rooted to the spot - unable to move - unable to think. Something obscene was crawling on top of Susan Jefferson.

Mohammed Jefferson lay there, bloated and enormous, like a leech that battens onto its prey and drains it of all vitality. He was wearing the remnants of an adult diaper that had long since burst from containing his bulk. Even now he wasn't much taller than the average six year old, but this only accentuated his inhuman girth.

As I watched, he suckled at his mother's shriveled breast as peacefully as a newborn baby.

Chun King's sister was watching me with eyes far too wise, a strange and distant smile dancing across her lips. When she spoke, it was with the passion of an apostle.

"It's my brother," she said. "Today's his birthday."

At the sound of her voice, the child-thing on the bed turned its eye upon me, pierced me with the malevolent gaze I remembered from before. There was a fire burning behind those eyes, a blistering acuity that scorched its way to the very core of who I believed myself to be.

The thing gazed at me, mother's milk and blood soaking his chins, and I was frozen.

It spoke to me, or at least it tried to. What came out of the open wound where its mouth should have been was little more than a strangled sob, a wet groan that trickled like rotten honey into my inner ear.

"You're the First," the girl said. "Bring them to us."

The sister extended her left arm toward the creature. That was when I noticed the scars. Her arm was covered with scabs, some old, some more recent. It took me a second to recognize them for what they were.

Bite marks.

The thing on the bed reared up and fastened its teeth into the girl's arm. A rivulet of blood dripped down onto the mattress, and pattered across the mother's stomach as Chun King sucked and nibbled at the girl's flesh.

The sister remained still; her empty gaze taking in everything and nothing. She might have been any American kid watching her favorite Saturday morning cartoon show. Reaching down with her right hand, she retrieved a half- empty bag of GORDITOS from the bed and began to eat.

The room shifted beneath my feet. A flush crept up the back of my neck, enveloping my eyes and head like a hood. There was no pain, merely an unfamiliar sensation of warmth. The last thing I remember is the two of them watching me, their eyes burning into mine.

Then I blacked out.

***

I returned to work the very next day. No fictional dead relative, no weekend withdrawal required. On Monday morning I felt as right as rain.

I do my job now. I find them. The freaks and misfits and "Super Fat Babies," the cold-eyed pederasts and gender-flipped sex fiends. I locate the lowest of the low and shove them out of the nest of anonymity and into the national spotlight of Morrie's modern day freak show.

But I work for another boss, one who holds a lot more than my immediate financial future in his hands.

He's building an army, you see.

At first, when the sister mentioned the "others" I had no idea who she meant. But by the time I made it back to Los Angeles I had pretty well figured it out.

The others. Others like him.

He's wearing us down. Understand? Destroying our sense of what is acceptable, sensible. And he's using the most powerful instrument of mass manipulation in the history of mankind to do it.

Watch the television sometimes and you'll see what I mean. But I warn you, the game's afoot. His numbers are growing and the Nielsen's have never been higher. Yesterday's show was called; "White Supremacist Meets Long Lost Mexican Son on Death Row!"

Our overnights are through the roof.

He's bigger now. He's waiting in that little house on the edge of that vast American desert, and he must weigh nearly four hundred pounds.

He's only seven years old.

I don't know how he got the way he is. Maybe he's a mutation. Or maybe he's an alien. The real deal, not one of the phonies we see on a monthly basis.

I buried Susan Jefferson in a dusty field outside San Bernardino. I believe she was intentionally placed in my studio, on my stage, as a lure. Chun King needs big numbers. That means television. He used his mother as bait to bring me into the fold.

The sister told me that their parents met while working in the nuclear waste processing plant out at the Air Force base. Maybe the answers to Chun King's origins lie in their radiation-riddled DNA. Their father, an Air Force sergeant, was killed in an accident at the plant soon after Mohammed's birth.

He has power. With a thought, he can cause pain or pleasure; pulses of delight that make me forget the things he compels me to do. I've seen him drive a man mad with a whisper.

That night, standing before them in that darkened room I felt that power. It thunders in my head even now, shatters my soul and makes me his creature. I feel the touch of his pleasure moving along the nerves of my spine like invisible butterfly wings and know that I am damned - a modern day Judas to the entire human species. And I am not alone.

All over the country there are others like him, more and more every day. They see my show, and they come to me. Across vast distances they come to me and through me...to Him.

And there are the folds: Folds of soft tissue that cover his body, all dermal elasticity gone from the incessant stretching of his skin. There are things nestled in the folds of his flesh, things that come out at night to feed.

The other day I interviewed a mother who videotaped herself murdering her seven children.

When I asked her why she did it, she said, "Why, for the talk shows of course."

Oh yes, my friends. They're out there.

I'm writing all of this down as a way of earning a measure of peace. When I'm done I intend to drop it in the nearest mailbox. It's addressed to an old Journalism professor of mine, a mentor. I think it will do the most good in his hands.

Chun King hates the human race that spawned him, the children that ridicule him on those rare occasions when he allows himself to be seen in public. He means to kill you or enslave you all, and remake the world in his own image.

After I make my little mail drop I'll go to my apartment. I have a gun there, a syndication gift from Morrie. I'm going to drive out to the little house in the desert and put an end to it, one way or another.

The sister never leaves his side. In her own way she has become as grotesque as he - speaking his word and will - the Oracle of a dark new god.

Several former Guests have moved in with them. One of them is a trucker from Tucson who sleeps with his daughter and can kill with a touch. One man claims to be the reincarnation of Jesus Christ, complete with toxic stigmata.

If can mask my thoughts long enough to get close to them, maybe I can use the gun. I had to hurt myself in order to interrupt the imposition of his will over my own.

I'm free for the moment.

Twenty minutes ago, I called in a few favors around town. If my plan pays off, the pain will have been worth it. Maybe I can direct the spotlight to where it will do some good. If I can kill enough of them before they kill me, the cameras will come. The cameras will always come. But if someone out there sees some part of the story, maybe enough real people will tumble to what's really happening.

As I close the envelope and seal it I savor the irony. I think about Susan Jefferson's face, and her wide, wide eyes. And as I turn out the lights in my office for the last time, I laugh.

What the Hell. Maybe my story will wind up on THE MORRIE STAPLER SHOW!

Michael Boatman

Michael Boatman

THE TARANTULA MEMOIRS

I was running scared. Believe me, when you can run at the speed of sound that's saying something. The prospect of meeting Prometheus face to face had me quivering in my black leather boots. Look. I'd stared Death in the eye on a daily basis, even before my retirement, but we're talking about a living breathing extraterrestrial here.[1] I suppose you could say that I was sort of a fan.

Prometheus had the strength of a thousand men. He had been credited with single-handedly bringing crime in Boston to a standstill. He could read minds, hear a butterfly beating its wings from his secret headquarters, which happened to be on the moon, plus he had a whole list of powers and abilities that put other M.V.s,[2] completely to shame.

His I.Q. was somewhere between "extraordinary genius" and the "I make Mensa members curl up in a corner and dribble" range. Plus he was handsome in the extreme, with the body and face of an African Adonis, and faster than a speeding ballistic missile.[3]

And he was immortal.

Prometheus had all this going for him, plus a great looking uniform whipped up for him by the Artificial Intelligence Servitors aboard the ship that had brought him here from the Great Beyond nearly seven decades earlier. I'm talking about the planet's

---

[1] Or extra-dimensional. I wasn't sure which at the time
[2] Masked Vigilantes, though I prefer 'Hyperheroes,' the term that Prometheus' girlfriend, Wanda Washington coined in the New York Clarion.
[3] The flying thing goes over like a dream with kids of all ages.

greatest defender; a beacon of strength, fairness and justice for all.

He wanted me to take down the King of the Fairies.

Now let me say one thing about that. It wasn't me that gave Oberon that title. It was Shakespeare who coined the term in A Midsummer Night's Dream. For those among you who haven't opened anything resembling a book since you dropped out of the sixth grade, Oberon was the King of the Fairies. Capische?

During our first battle atop the Empire State Building, that time I was on the trail of my arch-nemesis Ubermensch and Oberon stuck his cowled nose into things, I called him "Fairy King" because that was how I did things then: a little snappy patter to irritate and distract; then whammo! A few hundred subsonic uppercuts to the chops. How was I supposed to know the guy was the latest in a long string of costumed newcomers to set up shop in my hometown? Have you seen the New York skyline lately? It's busier than a cheap hooker on Saturday night.[4]

Okay, so Oberon got pissed and threw me over the side to plunge to my death a jillion stories below, right?

Wrong. Scratch that. If you'll study the numerous recordings of the battle, you'll discover that my going over was merely a ruse to distract the so called "Midnight Sleuth" while I reloaded my steel silk pods for another blast.

---

[4] Sorry, kids but as it says on the cover 'Adults Only.' The hyperhero game is not for the faint of heart and The Tarantula Memoirs are strictly for mommy and daddy.

And alright, Oberon did appear to leap over the side and shoot down one of his skim lines to grab me out of mid-air and haul me down to a lower floor where he set me down safe and sound with a stern warning about high places and name calling. I'll give him that. But I would have reloaded my steel silk shooters in another five seconds and saved myself. You can trust me on that one.

In any event, the two of us worked together a few times after that, several team-ups, during which we usually fought first but eventually managed to solve a crime or rescue a damsel in distress... but I never got to know the guy.

Let me explain something about hyperheroes. Not all of us are as open as yours truly: Jack Greer, once professionally known as The Tarantula! Dreaded, wall-walking Super Soldier of Hope, Happiness and the American Ideal!

Some of these people have real problems.

The whole secret identity thing for instance. I've never made any secret about my other career as a performance artist and painter. I've been famous, both as the Tarantula and as Jackson Greer. My parents, as everyone knows by now, were murdered by Ubermensch in the nuclear attack that gave me my powers. I've never been married. Well...not long enough to become a liability to my loved ones anyway. And I know of no little Tarantulas walking the walls of the city. Although with an ex-wife like mine who can say?

Despite my openness I've always been something of an outsider in the hyperhuman community. So imagine my surprise when I received an invitation, delivered to my PO Box and addressed to a Mr. T. Tula from Prometheus, the greatest Hyperhero of all time.

He was a legend by this time. Remember, he was the first one of us to step out of the shadows back in the early twentieth century. And by his own reckoning he was ancient even then, although he never looked a day over thirty five.

I had met and battled robots, mad dictators, terrorists of every stripe, creed and contour imaginable. I had fought the Mauler to a standstill with no steelsilk blasters to blind my foe or swing me out of harm's way.

But this guy was from another planet.

You've gotta understand the times we're talking about. By the second decade of the twenty-first century, the hyperhuman phenomenon had been well documented. The infamous "accident" at the Interdimensional Energies Project headed by Doctor Antonin Harris and his team out at Region 99, the Air force's most highly classified "non-existent" research facility, occurred at the height of WW II. It wasn't until the U.S. government sent their mysterious cadre of "mystery-men" into action against the Germans in 1943 that humanity became aware that the Age of the Superhuman had begun.

But there had been stories, as far back as the twenties, urban legends of a strange black man with silver eyes, who lived outside the normal conventions of the time. He appeared when needed most and always "in the pursuit of Justice," a phrase he himself made famous. With the evildoer incapacitated, he would vanish into the crowd.

At first he wore a simple black domino mask to conceal his features. But when the War ended, the Masked Vigilantes became the objects of distrust and fear rather than awe and inspiration. Prometheus was the first to appear in public without his mask, although he maintained the hyper-speed illusion that distorted his features. I've tried it. If you keep moving while standing still,[5] you can maintain a vibratory state wherein your features appear blurred to all but the sharpest superhuman eye.

So there I was, standing in my civs while people stared and snapped photos, reading a letter from the Mystery Man of the Future!

What I read had me shivering in my Birkenstocks:

T,
Oberon out of control. Please convene at Jo Rel's to discuss possibility of intervention.

Hoping this letter finds you well,

P.

P.S. Saw *Taking off the Mask* on satellite last night. Thought it was grand, though I doubt Medusa will approve.

I crumpled up the letter and stuffed it into my pocket as a kid stepped up and asked me for an autograph. For the first time since my "coming out" I felt a flash of irritation at this intrusion of fandom into my day-to day existence. If what I'd read was true, things were about to get ugly very, very soon. I wasn't at all sure I was up to it.

I took the pen from the kid and signed his book a little harder than I'd intended. The pen snapped in my grip and tore through the thick autograph book like a bullet through tissue paper.

"Hey!" the kid whined.

---

[5] Any speedster will know what I mean.

"Sorry 'bout that, son," I replied. I felt as if a dark shadow had slithered across the sun.

"That's ok, Tarantula," the kid smiled up at me.

"Hey, do you think you could...?"

Against my better judgment, I moved up and over the crowd that had gathered outside the post office. As they milled around, wondering where I'd gone, I made my way home, dizzy and reeling from my little disappearing act. But I had a lot of thinking to do before the meeting. I couldn't afford to be distracted.

The stakes were way too high.

***

We met at Jo Rel's the next day. But a gathering of well-wishers, tourists and wannabes forced us to move to a little table in the back near the kitchen. There, with Spanish music booming, I had my first face-to-face confrontation with the 'Man of Might.'

Looking at Prometheus - well - it's a little like seeing what might happen if the Clone Master got hold of Sidney Poitier, Arnold Schwarzennegger, Michael Jordan and threw in Albert Einstein's brain for kicks.

"Can I help you...gentlemen?" the waiter, a seedy DiCaprio type drawled. Jo Rel's was famous more for the attitude of its wait staff than for its hyperhuman customers. People in the Village are notoriously contemptuous of hyperheroes, largely because of our costumes; which they find abhorrent. All I know is that it sucks when you're battling Doctor Chaos below 23rd St and the people you're protecting stop to compliment *his* wardrobe.

We ordered gazpacho and a veggie platter. Prometheus raised a blurred eyebrow as he took in our surroundings.

"Are you certain coming out was the wisest thing to do, Jack?"

I jumped. Of course he knew my real name. The whole world knew my real name by then. Still. It sounded weird coming out of his mouth.

The waiter came by with our drinks and never batted an eyelash as Prometheus ordered a large salad with tofu, sprouts and black beans. That's the effect that blurring one's features has on civs. It tends to make them look the other way. Preoccupied human minds inevitably ignore what they can't perceive directly. The waiter simply looked through Prometheus instead of at him.

Man, this guy was good.

"Well, it seemed like a good idea after - after I retired," I said, somewhat lamely.

For some reason, I was suddenly ashamed. No. Prometheus made me feel ashamed, as if I'd betrayed a hyperhuman tradition simply by stepping fully into the public eye. But I was tired of playing "find the phone booth" while people died. I figured if there was a fire next door it was better to leap right in, rather than take precious seconds to change into my work duds.

"I simply meant..." he said as if he'd read my mind, "that I wonder if all this fuss is worth it. It must grow tiresome, being the object of such intense scrutiny."

Then Prometheus did something I didn't expect. He smiled and extended his right hand over the table.

"I meant no offence, Jack."

After a moment, I smiled back and accepted his hand. Hell, this guy had been pulling cats out of trees since before my grandfather was a kid. Who was I to take offence?

"None taken," I said. "So, what you wrote. Is it true?"

He stared at me a bit too long before he nodded gravely, as if he'd confirmed something for himself.

"The man I wrote to you about disappeared seven months ago. In all that time there have been no reported sightings of him in and around the Chicago area. Crime in the city has increased to record levels in his absence. Other hyperhumans like Carrion and the Scorcher have risen to fill the void left by his absence, but their effect on the growing crime wave has been minimal.

"It appears that word has gotten out among Chicago's criminal elite that the heat is effectively off, while other local heroes try to solve the mystery of where Oberon might have gone. Our colleagues in the Alliance are - concerned."

It sounded serious. Normally when one of us disappeared it was with good reason. Sometimes personal matters, family illness or the like, will take a hero off the streets. But the best ones always return. Just when you think they're down for good, they miraculously "return" just in time to save the day.

I, on the other hand, had officially retired from crime fighting. I'd saved thousands of lives, single-handedly saved the world more than a dozen times, and the known universe twice. I sipped at my iced tea to keep my hands from trembling. Prometheus sat there, studying me with his Ultra

Vision for all I knew. But I didn't care, because I knew by then, you see?

I knew that I was dying.

Civilians tend to think that people like me live forever. No one ever thinks a hero can die of an illness like radiation sickness.

"You said that he was out of control," I said, trying to take my mind off my own problems. "What makes you think he didn't retire, or go undercover? The Raven did it last year in San Francisco. It took her a whole year to infiltrate Johnny Skull's drug network. Maybe he's just keeping a low profile."

Prometheus shook his head. For just a moment he looked away, as if he didn't want to meet my eye. The tingle of fear I'd felt outside the post office returned. I wasn't sure I wanted to know whatever it was that could put a look like that on Prometheus's face.

He's not telling me everything, I thought. How bad is this going to get?

Then he reached into the leather satchel at his side, produced a thick envelope and laid it on the table.

"Our youngest member received these two weeks ago, while he was pursuing his nemesis through Chicago. He had to summon his other self to help him deal with the emotional trauma."

Prometheus pulled several photographs from the envelope.

"Leonard and...the subject were very close. He hasn't returned to us since."

I looked at the pictures, and I understood why little Lenny Arbogast had needed to summon the World's Strongest Samaritan. Each picture featured a man, at first it was hard to tell through the glaze of blood that covered him, one that I knew well enough

45

from my own encounters with him. And although Gordon Shockley, AKA the Gentleman, would go down as one of the most evil men in history, he couldn't have deserved the things that Oberon had done to him.

Shockley had been tortured. One set of photos featured the 'Midnight Sleuth' himself. In them, he had Shockley chained, with his back to a wall. Oberon stared directly into the lens, his piercing blue eyes glittering beneath the black cowl he wore to strike terror into the hearts of evil men. In another, Oberon's right hand held Shockley by the chin, his left fist pressed against Shockley's face in such a way that at first I didn't understand what I was seeing. There was so much blood, you see? But then I got it.

"Oh my God..."

Oberon had buried his forefinger up to the second knuckle in Shockley's eye socket. My gorge rose as I turned up the last and worst photo. It was the worst, not because of the depravity it contained, but because Oberon was smiling.

He had murdered Shockley and dismembered his corpse. The Midnight Sleuth grinned like a kid in a candy store. He'd painted the walls with Shockley's blood, hung his limbs from hooks, and used his entrails for bric-a-brac.

A message was attached to the photo. Written in a tight, precise script, the message told me everything I needed to know about Lenny Arbogast's breakdown.

"Dear Lenny,

That's right, I know who you really are you little shit, so listen up. I've got the secret ID's of every one of you meddlers in the Alliance of Justice. I know your strengths and your weaknesses better than you know them yourselves. You, for instance, can be dispatched by someone, say me for instance, sneaking in one night while you're sleeping and smashing your stupid, juvenile skull to fragments. All it takes is a well placed gag over your insipid little mouth to prevent you from crying out your ridiculous "magic word." Or maybe I'll just break your jaw and "Kazow!" No more Captain Wonder.

"Tell them, Arbogast. Tell Prometheus and the others that I'm doing things my way from now on. Tell them I'll kill everyone they ever cared about if they get in my way.

O

I dropped the photos on the table. I tried to focus my breathing as I'd been taught to do by Mind Storm after my initial diagnosis. Oberon had captured the Gentleman, one of Captain Wonder's greatest foes and subjected him to the most inhuman torture imaginable. Then he'd sent the pictures to a ten year old boy with the power of twelve gods.

"Each member of the Alliance received similar communications; delivered to our private residences," Prometheus said. "Each envelope contained images of one of our greatest foes, captured, tortured and murdered. I thought that, with your history having worked and fought with him in the past, I might coax you out of retirement for one last mission."

I barely heard Prometheus. One of the world's finest had gone to the "other side." No one, and I mean *no one* of Oberon's stature ever went over for long. Normally, in cases of mind control or some other unseen compulsion the big guns inevitably came back to their senses.

But the photos would not permit me the luxury of believing Oberon might be saved. Captain Wonder himself had been unable to capture the Gentleman. Oberon's skills as a hunter were clearly as sharp as ever, but his mind, once considered the greatest deductive intelligence on Earth, was now incomparably evil.

"You said he's done this to the others?" I whispered.

"Yes. He sent Medusa an email containing a photo of the Furies,"

He stopped. And for the second time that day, Prometheus did something that surprised me: He shuddered.

"I don't like to remember that there is such darkness on your world," he whispered. "Will you help us?"

I already knew my answer. I could no more have refused Prometheus than reverse the course of the disease that was slowly killing me.

Two years earlier, my final battle with Ubermensch atop the reactor at the San Rafael Nuclear Plant outside Los Angeles resulted in a containment breach of the reactor's core. I used a special compound in my steel silk blasters to contain the radiation until an emergency team could arrive to shut the reactor down, but I'd been required to stay and hold the web-seals in place for nearly an hour. I'd saved the city. But I'd overtaxed my hyperhuman resistance to radiation once too often.

My doctor, a discrete associate at Tech-Gen Laboratories gave me the dreary prognosis a year later. As of this writing I probably have a year before the radiation takes its final toll.

The irony is that my hyperhuman metabolism repels all attempts to save my life. The sickness has mutated and integrated with my powers. You could stab me and I'd heal fast enough to chase you down and make you regret it, but the thing that's going to kill me is eating away at me from the inside.

I'd intended to spend my retirement writing books and consulting on movies about my hyperhuman adventures. I had no desire to expend whatever courage I had left pursuing costumed lunatics bent on blowing up the world.

"Why did you come to me?" I asked. "You know I'm retired. Why not the Mauler? Or the Raven? She's at least as powerful as I am."

Prometheus looked at me for a long moment. When he finally spoke it was with great care.

"The Raven is dead, Jack. She encountered Oberon outside Milwaukee after he'd murdered a trainload of federal prisoners."

Horror sank its talons into the lining of my gut. The Raven was an old friend. And at one time, as I've written elsewhere in these memoirs, she was more than that. At one time, we were engaged.

I excused myself, stood up and went to the bathroom. When I returned I ordered a drink. Prometheus noted this with another raised eyebrow but said nothing.

"You should understand one thing before I commit to helping you," I said. "My powers aren't what they once were. I may not be much help to the Alliance."

Prometheus smiled.

"I think you may be just what the Alliance needs," he said. "There's more than one kind of power, Jack."

And just like that, I had it, the reason why a man who could fly at the speed of light might require the aid of a dying, mid-level human superhero: The Alliance was filled with beings who, like Prometheus, were the stuff of legends: a boy with godlike abilities; a woman who wielded the powers of a mythological demon, androids, magicians. All of them were damn near immortal, invulnerable or both.

But I wasn't.

"How's your health insurance plan?" I said.

The old banter felt right somehow. Hell, it was the first joke I'd made in a long while. My new partner smiled again. And I realized that Prometheus understood what makes human beings tick better than anyone might have believed possible.

I took the envelope and slid it into my own satchel. I could feel the old curiosity kicking in, and the familiar compulsion to right a great wrong. One of the world's most powerful heroes had become one of its most dangerous villains. It was up to the Alliance to put him down.

It would be a good way to die.

I thought about the ancient Viking berserkers, men who'd held contempt for the warrior who died the "straw death," wasting away in his bed, rendered irrelevant by old age or sickness, rather than dying on the field of battle.

Yes. An excellent way to die.

But then I remembered little Lenny Arbogast, hovering in the nowhere dimension he inhabited whenever he summoned his mighty alter ego. I thought about the suffering that Oberon had inflicted on an evil man, and the murder of a good woman with whom I'd danced across a thousand moonlit rooftops...

And I thought it might also be an excellent way to live.

THE DROP

Cyrell Biggs was just about to pop Buster Plump upside the head when the Colored Mermaid stuck her head out of Lake Armstrong and gave him the finger.

Cyrell dropped the lug wrench Moniqua Plump had given him to "beat the fat dog killer's brains out" with.

"Goddamn it!" Buster said. "Where'd he go?"

"Boss, I just saw..." Cyrell said.

"Stanky Methuselah," Buster said. "Biggest catfish anyone in this lousy town ever seen smelled or heard of. I had him hooked."

Cyrell tapped Buster on the shoulder on account of he was looking in the wrong direction. The Mermaid was still there, bobbing about twenty feet from where they floated in the Sweet Minnie, Buster's tired little dinghy.

She held one elegant black arm out of the water and extended her middle finger.

Why, she's ugly as two-week-old bladder panties, Cyrell thought.

He thumped Buster again. "Look!"

"What, man?" Buster said.

The Colored Mermaid dove. Cyrell saw that long black tail uncurl, its flukes glistening in the moonlight, before she sank out of sight.

"I saw her," he said. "She - It - daaahhhh."

Buster rolled his eyes - and his chins - and smacked Cyrell upside his head. The smack startled a nearby heron, who uttered a suggestive squawk and took off.

"C - Colored Mermaid," Cyrell gasped. "I saw the Colored Mermaid."

53

Still scowling, Buster glanced out over the water. The freckles on his nose twitched, then his eyes squeenched up even tighter.

"Well now," he said. "You might be right."

Cyrell ogled Buster like a neutered coonhound with a new set of nuts.

"You believe me, Boss?"

"Hell yes," Buster said. "Seen her myself once."

He glared at the patch of black water from whence the mermaid had flipped them off. "She probably stole Ol' Stanky right off my hook!"

Something big splashed in the dark.

"Anytime you're ready, honey!" Buster hollered.

"When's the first time you seen her?" Cyrell said.

Buster belched.

"Back when I was fifteen. Me and my daddy was night fishin' over the Drop."

Cyrell shuddered. Everyone in Pepper's Flip, Louisiana Pop. 1643 knew about Lake Armstrong and the Drop.

"My daddy told me it's almost a mile deep, Cyrell said.

"Your daddy was stupider than you are," Buster said. "They got a network of bottomless caves down there. You swim down too deep and you'll wake up in Hong Kong with lava shootin' out your ass."

"Yeah?" Cyrell said.

"Drop's never been measured though," Buster said. "Cuz nobody gives a raggedy goddamn."

"I heard the ghosts of lynched runaway slaves be walkin' round down there," Cyrell said, breathlessly. He knew he'd come out here to do something but he'd forgotten what it was. "When the moon is full and the mist gets heavy you can hear them screamin'."

Buster snorted. "Screamin' for what?"

Cyrell glanced around before answering. "Human flesh."

"Hmmmmph," Buster grunted.

"I heard the FBI even come out here lookin' for UFO's back in '77," Cyrell said.

"Awww bullshit," Buster said. He produced one of his hand-rolled Dominican cigars and lit up. "Wasn't no flyin' saucer snatched my pap. Colored Mermaid done that. I seen it."

"She took Big Pooty?" Cyrell said. "But you told me he got drunk and run off with the Panther Girl from the African Soul Circus."

Buster plopped his butt down, plucked a fifty-ounce bottle of Black Ram out of the cooler and cracked it open.

"I lied."

The night heaved a warm sigh.

"Snatched my daddy out this very boat," Buster said. "Same way your Mama snatched the wig off Loquatia Jenkins's head down at the Uppity Crab."

Cyrell winced as Buster brayed. Mama out-drank men three times her weight in that same establishment most Saturday nights. He dog-paddled through another blast of Buster's ridicule; a sooty waft of cheap beer and cigar smoke hecatombed the hairs in his nostrils.

"You know what I enjoy?" Buster said. "Drinkin' beer, smokin' cigars and stompin' a mudhole in yo' stupid ass."

Nearby, a geriatric skunk soiled its nest. Cyrell's excitement faded into the crappy backdrop against which the rest of his miserable life was set.

"No one except me is gonna believe you seen the Mermaid," Buster said. "Nobody'd give a damn no how."

Cyrell nodded. In a town full of broke Blacks, poor Mexicans, indigent Indians and White Trash, Cyrell Biggs had the bottom of the totem pole all to himself.

"Cousin," Buster observed. "You ain't just dumb. You got the double distinction of bein' ignorant too."

"I ain't bright," Cyrell said.

"Boy, you make Junebug Bicks look like a road scholar. And he been brain dead since they fished his ass outta this lake."

Cyrell nodded. Everybody knew the story of how Junebug got drunk one night and took a header off Ellington Pier; when they found Junebug lying face down on the shore a few hours later, he'd been bled half-dry from slashes on his chest and thighs and some other places that made Cyrell squeeze his knees together if he thought about it too much.

"Cyrell," Buster said. "You're worse than dumb. You're nigga dumb, and that's ten times dumber than regular dumb."

Buster cracked Cyrell across the back of the head - THWAAK! - and Cyrell's last piece of strawberry Bubble-rific bubble gum shot out of his mouth and hit the water with a loud *plunk!*

"I'm talkin' to you, man!"

"Sorry, Boss," Cyrell said.

"I din't become owner of Buster's Barbecue Empire to be disrespected by an ungrateful asshole like you."

"Sorry, Boss."

"You ain't sorry yet," Buster said. "But you gonna be."

Cyrell blinked. "What?"

"Take us out," Buster said. "Catfish bite better over the Drop."

As he turned away, Buster's penny loafer snagged the business end of Moniqua's lug wrench.

"What the hell is that doin' here?"

Cyrell grabbed the wrench, trying to ignore the flush of guilt burning up the back of his neck. Buster was glaring at him the way a night owl eyes a back-broke rat.

Happily ever after, muchacho.

The thought of Moniqua waiting set Cyrell's heart a 'flutter. *You make sure he's good and drunk,* she'd told him. *Then pop him and dump him.*

Cyrell steered the Sweet Minnie toward deep water. He coughed, trying to hide the secret little smile he got whenever he thought about the way he loved Moniqua. *'Specially that little noise she makes when we're mem-o-ratin Chin Chin,* he thought.

Moniqua's dog Chin Chin was the reason Cyrell got lucky three nights a week behind the animal shelter out on Route 9.

"Buster threw my baby into a cremation canister while he was sleeping," Moniqua told Cyrell one day. "Fat son-of-a-bitch paid the Animal Control man a hundred bucks to take a long lunch while my Chin Chin burned."

Sometimes Moniqua wanted to "commemorate" the little Shih-Tzu on top of all seven cremation canisters. Sometimes Cyrell had to limp home after commemorating Chin Chin all night long.

Oh yeah.

Moniqua didn't seem to mind that the Lord Jesus Christ had given Cyrell the brain of a half dead Chinese jackass. Then again, Cyrell figured there was one hacked off Asian burro gunning for the man who got his cock & balls to boot.

Ay, muchacho, Moniqua said, the night they christened Chin-Chin's canister. *That's a lotta chorizo.* The Lord had been good to Cyrell in that respect.

Around that time, Shed Wilbon - the ex-con who fixed trucks down at Hy's Auto Repair - came sniffing around. Pretty soon he and Moniqua started carrying on like they were sharing a dirty little joke without letting Cyrell in on the punchline.

THWACK!

"I said hand me another beer!" Buster said. "You'd best pull your head outta your ass, Cyrell Biggs."

Buster unleashed a gastric detonation that offended a family of gators lounging in the reeds. Caught unawares, the big bull performed an involuntary "death roll," righted himself and sank quietly out of sight.

Buster was glaring at Cyrell in that strange, hungry way again. Then he looked out over the water.

"You don't see her when she gets you," he said. "Night she took Big Pooty, I only caught a flash of that black tail slidin' around my daddy's throat like a big wet cottonmouth. Then he was gone."

"Jeeesus," Cyrell said. "Would' a been neat to set a eyeball on her. Like that goat sucker they got down in..."

Cyrell's voice tapered off. Then he shot to his feet.

"Hey, Boss! You think they might could put me on one of them TV shows about para-natural experiences?"

Buster cussed and belched at the same time.

"God-bhrraaapp your ignorant ahhrrauuggg, Cyrell. Some amphibulous whore snatches my lovin' daddy and makes me an orphan. What the hell's so 'neat' about that?"

"I just..."

"Boy,'bout the only thing more mentally inert than you *might* be a bag o' hammers," Buster said. "And that slut I married, of course."

"Don't..." Cyrell rasped before he could stop himself. But Buster was rolling and he didn't notice.

"Between you and that no account egg sack it's a wonder I ain't treated myself to a tri-state killing spree."

Hit him, Cyrell thought. *Shut that fat mouth once and for all.*

"Reckon I'll start with Moniqua," Buster said. "Gut her like the hog she is and put my wallet outta its misery."

Cyrell chewed his bottom lip, swallowed liquid iron.

"Hand me my goddamn rod," Buster said. "Came out here to catch me some catfish and here I sit, talkin' to a natural born fool."

Cyrell stood there with blood dribbling down his chin.

"Oh, move outta my way, dummy."

Buster shoved Cyrell out of the way and bent over.

Cyrell drew out the wrench. He gripped it with both hands and raised it the over his head. Then he closed his left eye and drew a bead on the hole in Buster's afro.

"I know you two been doin' it," Buster said.

Cyrell's eye popped open.

"What?"

Buster stood up. Instead of his fishing rod, he was pointing his Redhawk .44 Magnum at Cyrell's nuts.

"Y'all must think I'm stupid too," Buster said.

"Uhhh..."

"I got eyes everywhere, Cyrell. Ears too."

"Wait..." Cyrell said.

"Got me a certain lady friend who uses special equipment to keep up with Queen Moniqua when I'm gone."

"Special equipment?" Cyrell whispered.

"Video, Cy," Buster said. "I got forty hours of you and my wife humpin' like rats." He lifted the Redhawk. "You stabbed me in the back, motherfucker."

African terror teamed up with Baptist guilt and sucker punched Cyrell in the kidneys. He raised his other hand, the one without the wrench.

"I - I have to pee," he whispered.

"Show it to me."

Cyrell froze. "What you say?"

Buster stepped closer, his eyes hooded, a hulking silhouette in the half-light of the full moon.

"Show me what she's been cheatin' for, Cyrell, or I'll put a bullet through it."

Buster thumbed back the hammer on the Redhawk - CLICK - and Cyrell reached down with his left hand, unzipped his pants and let them fall to his feet. Buster stared for a long time. Finally, he nodded.

"You two was 'bout the only family I had in this world," he said. "That's a sorry ass thing for a man like me to admit to a man like you. Pull them britches up."

Cyrell complied. Meanwhile the malignant puffer fish living in his bladder giggled and doubled its size.

"We gonna settle this like men," Buster said. "If you win, you get the girl. I don't hold no grudges."

Cyrell's brain was screaming around the inside of his skull like a Hot Wheels racer on a bright orange plastic loop-de-loop.

"What if you win?" he said.

Buster waggled the Redhawk.

"Me and Moniqua gonna make our own video," he said. "Something featurin' a lot of close-ups of my foot breakin' off in her ass."

Cyrell's racer flipped off the track.

He'd had Moniqua every way that lust, opportunity and business hours at the animal shelter allowed. He couldn't have been more busted if he'd filled himself with helium and tried to float up a porcupine's ass- crack.

"You - can't - hurt her." he said.

"You and me gonna settle up fair and square," Buster said. "Soon's you drop that nigger-beater."

Cyrell's eyes narrowed. Buster was as slow as molasses in January when he wasn't drunk, and he made Cyrell do all the heavy lifting at work. Cyrell, on the other hand, could move like good gossip when he wanted to.

A smile flickered at the corners of his mouth: He was beginning to think he might finish the evening with the same number of testicles he began it with. He dropped the lug wrench and raised his fists.

"I been fightin' since I'm two years old," Cyrell said.

"That's true," Buster grinned. "Fightin' common sense."

Buster smirked. Then he shot Cyrell in the chest.

"Fair and square!" Cyrell screamed as he fell. "You said fair and square!"

Buster grinned and kicked him in the nuts.

"Didn't build a culinary empire so some half-Mexican whore and her back stabbin' retard could take it away."

Then he stooped and grabbed the lug wrench.

"Been good to you, Cyrell. Ever since mama made me play with you 'cuz you was feeble in the head."

Buster raised the monkey wrench and brought it down hard on Cyrell's right kneecap. Cyrell howled.

"I gave you a job, man," Buster said. "Good job too."

Buster belched and smashed Cyrell's other kneecap. Cyrell whooped in a great shuddering breath to scream. The hole in his chest whistled Dixie.

He scuttled backward, his legs dragging behind him through the blood trail he left in his wake. Buster minced through the blood, hoisted his left foot...

"Smilin' faces tell lies..."

...and brought three-hundred and fifty pounds of beer, barbecue and bullshit down on Cyrell's ankle.

"Snap. Crackle. Pop," he said.

Pain put on a Fourth of July Extravaganza in Cyrell's brain. He heaved his upper body up onto the side and stretched his right hand out over the water.

"Comin' - comin' to save you, honey," he said.

Blood droplets dripped from his fingers like rubies thrown into the abyss. The droplets left a thin black film on the surface for a moment. Then they were absorbed.

"Cold - Hurts," Cyrell gasped.

Buster's beard stubble scraped his left ear.

"Ain't even a piece of what I'm gonna do to your girlfriend, Cy."

"Don't - don't hurt her," Cyrell said.

Far below them, a ripple of light flickered in the depths of the lake. Buster didn't see the light, not even when, a moment later, it flickered again, closer this time. But Cyrell saw it.

Something was rising toward them.

"Help me," Cyrell whispered.

"I tried to help you, asshole."

Buster grabbed Cyrell and head butted him. Cyrell staggered and almost fell over the side, but Buster grabbed him. He lifted Cyrell off his feet and crushed him to his chest in a bear hug.

"Ooopppshh," Cyrell said.

Buster looked down: Two of Cyrell's teeth clung to the pocket of his Walmart XXXtra-Portly bowling shirt.

"Xtra-Portly my ass," Cyrell giggled.

Buster went crazy then. He beat Cyrell with his fishing rod; beat him some more with the wrench; even busted a full Black Ram upside his head. Finally, when he'd run out of blunt objects, Buster shoved his head underwater.

Cold rushed in and shoved twin railroad spikes up Cyrell's nose. His ruptured lung didn't permit the luxury of holding his breath; he sucked ice instead. Stupid, he thought.

Ignorant.

Mentally inert.

Idiot.

Then he saw her.

Through water as black as the heart of midnight she rose, shimmering like the memory of a childhood dream.

The Mermaid slid between bright beams of moonlight, slipping into shadow one moment, aglow with mutant sea shine the next. Ghost lights danced along fan-like ridges lining her skull and spine. Her eyes shone like pearls in the gloom. Her skin was the color of pitch, smooth and scaled like the new hide of a great black serpent.

Buster hauled Cyrell half out of the water.

"We're right over the Drop, cousin." he said. "But don't worry. You'll have company down there real soon."

Then Buster let him go. Cyrell tried to swim but his legs were dead stumps and he sank like a stone.

Goodbye, Monie-love, he thought.

But instead of sinking Cyrell was rising, pulled upward in the Mermaid's wake. Her momentum slammed him against the hull of the Sweet Minnie. A moment later, his head broke the surface.

"You might'a got my pap, but you ain't gettin' me!"

It was Buster.

Cyrell clawed his way up the side of the boat. He managed to grab Buster's cooler but the top flipped up and smacked him in the mouth.

Stupid.

Stupid.

Stupid.

Cyrell held on anyway.

Above him in the Sweet Minnie, Buster's Redhawk went off. The explosion seized the muscles in Cyrell's neck like a vise. Buster's second shot tore the air over his head. Cyrell heard a sound like a sharpened Louisville Slugger punching through a sack of pig guts and Buster squealed.

"Hurts! Ahhhhhhh, that huuurrts!"

Cyrell closed his eyes, but he couldn't block out those sounds: neckbone twisting, frogleg sucking sounds that pan-fried the meat between his ears; couldn't do anything except cling to the Sweet Minnie until the sounds stopped and his strength gave out.

Then he let go.

Safe now, he thought, as the waters closed over his head. *Safe now.*

Cyrell took that with him, down into the dark.

He awoke to the sound of teeth grinding against bone. The pain in his legs was gone. Cyrell looked down and he understood why.

Buster's corpse gaped up at him from the weeds covering the sandy bottom. His throat, chest and stomach, torn open, made feasting places for the mermaid's children.

Nearly three dozen semi-human shapes arrowed through the water, their cries filling Cyrell's head with clicks and moans.

A young female, half Cyrell's size, rose to peer at him. Her skin was pale, her eyes twin pearls. Something that was not hair surrounded her head; a white flurry of thin tendrils. The feelers reached for Cyrell but with a flick of her head, the little mermaid pulled them back. The glowing edge of her tail sliced once at the skin on Cyrell's bare chest and withdrew.

She was carrying Buster's face in her hands, black claws hooked through empty eye sockets.

The Colored Mermaid floated out of the darkness. She was nearly invisible in the shadows save for the burning streamer of red mist rising from two holes between a double row of nipples lining her chest: crimson testament to Buster's marksmanship.

The children encircled her, grasping, darting in and out of the incandescent blood cloud through which she drifted; singing.

She was singing for Cyrell.

Her voice was the cold whisper of eels; her song a dirge, the requiem for a dead and distant sea. She sang of debt and duty, of endings and beginnings. Cyrell moved, drawn forward by her song.

Shining spines flexed along the muscular silver tail that extended from his lower torso. He pumped the new appendage and felt its coiled power propel him closer to her. Cool currents slithered over naked new flesh as he swam, moving as she moved, at one with the black water. They joined. His spines lifted, engorged, and pierced the flesh between the mermaid's shoulder blades. She screamed. Teeth sharp enough to pierce bone bit into the knot of muscle at the joining place between Cyrell's neck and shoulder.

They hovered there, limbs and tails entwined, while the water around them burned.

And Cyrell understood it all.

He smelled the woman before she saw him.

Startled, Moniqua dropped her cool drink. The tinkle of shattering glass was a symphony in Cyrell's ears.

"I thought you wasn't coming back, muchacho," she said.

He tasted her confusion; old lemon and dark chocolate. She hadn't counted on facing him alone. But Shed Wilbon lay a few yards away, his spine shattered, his last cigarette burning the webbing between his broken fingers.

"Is it done?" she said.

"It's over," he said.

Cyrell stood in the shadows sifting the dregs of human desire from the air of Buster's Barbecue, the smell of grease from the cold grills, Moniqua's musk mingled with Shed's cologne and the iron bite of gunpowder.

"Why don't you come inside, where I can see you, Cy?"

"I want to show you something," he said. "Come walking with me."

His fingers twitched. The legs he wore would only last while the moon shone upon the waters of the lake, and the children hungered for the things he could provide.

For them. For her.

"You're scaring me, Cy," she said.

Cyrell nodded, tasting her fear now.

"I know."

He stepped into the light and Moniqua screamed. Love, the first he'd ever known, had made a new man of him.

Wise now, Cyrell began to sing.

KATCHINA

My husband is not a monster.

Leona Brinkmore stared at the photographs. The twelve pictures of murdered women could have been fakes.

Why would Lester fake something like this, Leona?

Many of the women looked like Leona - brown skinned, black or Hispanic women. Some looked underfed. Some were missing teeth. All of them had been strangled, their eyes swollen shut beneath bruised folds of flesh. Someone had bashed the women's faces in.

A sound from the bedroom made Leona jump.

She dropped the pictures back into the little space under the floor in Lester's closet, her heart thundering in her chest. If he found her there, rooting through his 'personals' he would beat her.

She peeped around the corner into their bedroom. She half expected him to be standing there. But she was alone.

Been alone since the day your daddy gave you to Doctor Lester Brinkmore, a voice reminded Leona.

She closed her eyes, forced herself to breathe.

She reached back into the hole in the floor.

Some of the dead women were naked, or only partially clothed. In one photo, the woman had been posed, her head tilted back to expose her throat. The angry bruises around her neck shouted accusations.

There were other things in the hole: a pair of silver eyeglasses with one lens smashed, a single gold hoop earring with dried blood on the clasp. And a doll.

The doll was a tiny replica of an Indian baby, wrapped in a red and white blanket. A lock of black hair had been attached to its head. Leona had seen similar dolls in the shops inside the Indian casinos across the Lake in Michigan.

This is a Katchina, Leona thought. *Yes that's right.*

They'd visited the Indian shops when Lester took her to Michigan on their honeymoon. Sometimes the Indian women adorned the dolls with locks of their own hair to entreat the spirits to protect their newborn babies.

Leona stared at the doll and the pictures until her vision swam and her head ached. It took her a moment to realize that the alarm clock on the stove was chiming.

She wiped her eyes. Lester was due in from the hospital any minute. If he found she'd cooked his porterhouse too long or not enough...if it wasn't exactly the way he liked it, she would suffer for it.

Leona put the doll and the pictures back in the hole.

She'd finished shining Lester's shoes the same way she'd done once every week for the last twelve years. But when she'd set them down in their usual spot, on the floor in the back of his closet behind his suits, one of the floorboards had come loose. Leona had pushed down on the floorboard and found the hollow space beneath.

Then she'd seen the pictures.

Like a cry for help, she thought.

Leona pushed such thoughts away, put them away with the terrible faked pictures. The stove was chiming again.

She went and got Lester's dinner.

70

Ivy Horse dragged herself out of the mass grave she shared with eleven other corpses. The Pain, like a ringing shriek in her mind, refused to leave her in peace. She coughed up the pebbles and dirt her killer had forced her to swallow before he'd strangled her, and climbed out of the hole into which he'd tossed her like so much trash.

She didn't see the rude staircase that led up to the first floor of the fire gutted old house. Rats had taken her right eye the second night of her internment. The Pain guided her feet toward the stairs. As she walked through the halls of the dark old house, the Pain sang to her. As she stepped out into the moonlight the Pain told her who she'd been:

the granddaughter of African slaves and Seminole Indians, descended from the Florida tribes who fled Southern hatred during the Great Northern Migration of the nineteen-thirties and forties.

She'd been poor. During the toughest times she'd hooked a little to pay the bills. She'd promised herself a million times that she would stop; Just one more "date." But two part time jobs weren't always enough. Then she'd met Joe, a good man who treated her well. Together they'd fallen, and she quit the life for good.

A few months later, they'd gotten the good news.

They'd decided to leave the City. Chicago was no longer the Great Northern Dream it had been for their parents. A housing project was no place to raise a family. She'd been on her way out to her parents' house in Hammond when her car quit on her. The last thing she remembered was starting at the sharp rap on her window. And the successful looking black man who asked if she needed help.

The Pain comforted her as she walked alongside the dark stand of trees that bordered the highway, not far from where her car had broken down exactly one month ago.

Ivy Horse walked on into the darkness, listening.

The Pain was instructive about many things.

***

Lester hit Leona so hard that her eyes rolled back into her head; for a moment she thought she was going to black out.

"You think I owe you anything, you dumb monkey?" he snarled. "You think I owe you another day of breathin' my air and walkin' on my floors?"

"No, Lester," Leona said.

"Every morning I go out of this house and take care of people who call me 'nigger' behind my back."

"Yes, Lester."

"Last thing I need is you naggin' me about where I've been and who I've been with."

Lester let her go. Leona half staggered/half fell trying to get away from him.

He'd come in two hours late from the hospital. In a panic, she'd done everything she knew to keep his porterhouse from drying out. But he'd come in stinking of expensive whiskey, sat in front of the television and eaten his dinner without a word to her.

Leona thought about the pictures. The women with their heads tilted up. The bruises on their throats. *He's gonna kill you, fool.*

Her thoughts were interrupted by the blare of sound from the television.

"...police have bee been hard-pressed to come up with any leads in the disappearances of a dozen women from the Alderman-Brody housing developments and the surrounding area. Terrified residents of the 'projects' are calling for an investigation."

Leona carried Lester's TV tray over to the sink. Her attention wandered to the picture on the television screen. A moment later, the tray clattered to the floor.

The woman in the photograph looked only a few years younger than Leona, no older than twenty-five. She was beautiful, with long black hair and

73

wide, laughing black eyes. In the photograph she stood next to a smiling older couple, whom she resembled.

"...the most recent to go missing, Ivy Horse, a South side resident who vanished last month. Horse, who is twenty-three years old, is expecting a child later this month. Tonight, Mayor Dee, along with Ivy's family is asking for your help. If you know anything about these disappearances..."

Lester leaned forward in his chair, his eyes shining, and turned up the volume. Moving automatically, Leona cleaned the remnants of his dinner off the floor and scraped them into the disposal unit. Her daddy, a fundamentalist Baptist preacher, had trained her up right, long before Lester came along.

Girl, you're too funny-lookin' to make a proper wife. Better learn your way 'round the kitchen if you wanna catch a half-way decent husband.

She loaded the dishwasher without paying attention, unable to look away. Pictures showing five of the missing women flashed on the screen. Leona didn't know any of them.

But she recognized all of them.

The pain in the back of her neck made her cry out.

"I told you to get me a beer."

Lester had her by her ponytail. He jerked her head back and snarled into her ear. "What's wrong with you?"

"I...I..." she stammered, unable to think. "I..."

"You what?"

Leona glanced down at the dishwasher. She'd left the door open, the machine half-filled.

The big butcher knife lay on the top shelf.

74

It would be so easy, she thought.

But aloud she said, "I'm sorry, Lester."

He slapped her, once, sharply across the face.

Then he dragged her into the bedroom and raped her.

***

Ivy Horse limped along dark streets she could never have afforded to traverse when she was alive. Her killer had been particularly cruel. Her left arm had been pulled nearly out of its socket. In his rage, he'd shattered her right cheekbone. Her head hung at the wrong angle from where he'd wrung her neck. But the Pain distracted her from these minor hurts. The Pain giggled. Then it told her to stop.

Ivy stopped. The thing she sought was inside the immaculate yellow house. The Pain told her so.

Ivy dragged herself up the walkway.

***

Leona couldn't sleep. She sat at the kitchen table staring at the pictures from Lester's closet. Lester was upstairs, snoring with his legs on her side of the bed. He'd choked her nearly unconscious before forcing himself on her. Now her body felt like one big bruise.

She'd inherited the immaculate yellow house. Her mother had died giving birth to her and her father had spent the rest of his life making sure Leona never forgot. Lester's childhood home was on the other side of Garvey, near the abandoned steel mill. It had burned to the ground five years ago.

Lester's parents had made him the executor of their estates after they went into the senior complex over in Riverglen, but Lester had never seen fit to repair the old place. It sat like the ruined wrack of Leona's marriage, a blackened husk, empty of light.

A noise from outside made Leona look up from the pictures. Lately, an old raccoon had been raiding the trash bins next to the back door. Leona got up and went to the window above the sink. It looked out over the trash bins in the backyard. A tap on the window usually scared the raccoon away.

The back yard was empty. Bright moonlight, sharp as a scalpel's edge illuminated the patio and the pool. Only the interior of the garage remained thick with shadows. Lester had left the door up again.

Too drunk, Leona thought.

She drew her robe tight and unlocked the back door. Lester would expect to find the garage closed and locked when he left for work in the morning. If she didn't do it now, she'd regret it later.

Fool, her mind warned. *There won't be a later for you.*

Leona crossed the driveway. She walked to the touchpad on the outer wall of the garage. Lester had installed it so he could open the door manually using a numeric code.

Last chance. Drive away and never look back.

"Where would I go?" she asked the cold night wind.

All of her people were dead. She had no one to run to, no real education, no money of her own. Everything was in a joint account that Lester controlled.

Leona entered the code, 2-24-61, Lester's birthday, and stepped back as the garage door rolled down and clicked against the driveway. She pulled her robe tightly around her shoulders, shivering at the chill that trickled down the back of her neck.

Then she went back inside.

***

"Dalton Police department. How can I help you?"

Leona almost hung up the phone. Her fingers flickered along the flat contours of the brown girl's picture, the wide brow; the cheekbones high and sharp as a mother's curse. The girl's smile had been corrupted by agony, reforged into a grimace.

"Dalton Police Department. How can I help you?"

"I know..." Leona stammered. "I know what happened...to those girls."

"Who is this?"

"I need help," Leona whispered, then with greater force, "Help me."

The sound of footsteps froze the words on her lips. Leona turned, her mind whirling.

Lester was leaning over the kitchen table. Leona's mouth went dry and the phone dropped from her fingers.

"Hello?" the telephone said. Then the line went dead.

Half shrouded in the moonlight, Lester seemed intent upon the items she'd stolen from his closet. He studied them closely, his nose pressed to the table.

Alright then, she thought. *Alright then.* She reached out and grabbed the butcher knife.

The figure at the table stood and Leona saw that it was not Lester. The woman - yes it was a woman - her face was lost behind the veil of black hair that hung almost to the table.

"Who are you?" Leona hissed. "What do you..."

The woman stepped into the beam of moonlight shining through the kitchen window and Leona fell silent. Even with all that Lester had done to her Ivy Horse's smile remained. She held up the thing she'd taken from the kitchen table.

"Kat...chi...na," she moaned.

The dead woman caressed the bulge that protruded from her exposed midsection, caressed it as a mother caresses the cheek of a sleeping infant.

The bulge moved. The woman's belly rippled, her flesh roiling like the surge on a sluggish sea. Leona's mouth stretched wide, a scream beating its way up from deep inside her gut. Her hand gripped the handle of the butcher knife.

The shadow/woman turned and walked out the back door.

"Wait," Leona hissed. "Stop!"

Heedless, Leona followed the dead woman from the house and down the back stairs. The woman walked swiftly, her legs ticking like a windup doll. She marched toward the woods.

Lena followed. The curve of the woman's spine brooked no denials. Her will accepted no delusions. She had defied Death itself to gain her desire: That strength drew Leona on. She ran through the woods until the dead woman walked into the clearing that faced Lester's childhood home. Leona stepped into the clearing and Ivy vanished, swallowed by the old house.

Something rustled in the woods behind her.

The flame that had fueled her flight shuddered and grew dim. Fear pushed her across the clearing and over the threshold. Leona stumbled over the landing in the darkness, lost her footing and fell headlong down the stairs. She hit the dirt floor and felt something tear in her right shoulder. She bit back her scream, sensing that she'd blundered into a sacred place.

She caught a glimpse of the dead woman climbing down a hole in the floor. Leona stood - the movement slicing jagged ripples across the muscles of her back and shoulder - and picked her way through the dark until she reached the hole. She looked into that abyss but could see only darkness.

"Maybe you aren't as stupid as you look."

He was on her before she could turn. Lester punched her in the kidneys and Leona felt something with blades unfold itself in her lower back.

"You woke me up, monkey," he growled. "You know better than that."

Leona lifted her left hand. In the darkness Lester didn't see his danger. She drove the butcher knife into the big muscle of his left thigh.

Lester uttered a surprised yelp of pain. Leona raised her left hand again and slammed the knife into his left buttock. Howling, Lester punched her, knocked her to the dirt floor. The knife spun away in the darkness. Lester straddled her chest, grabbing for her throat.

Leona clawed stripes of flesh from his face, hooked her fingernails into the soft tissue of one eye. His pain had ignited something in her blood, something black of heart and red of claw, and she screamed: "Killyou! I'llkiiillyooouu!"

Lester's hands found her throat and began to squeeze. Leona's heartbeat thundered in her ears, filled the world with its pounding rush. Her vision flashed white, flickered and darkened.

Then Lester screamed, and the air turned cold. Gasping, Leona looked up. Twelve corpses surrounded them in the half-light.

Ivy Horse had buried Leona's butcher knife between Lester's shoulder blades. Moving as one, the women bent and picked up jagged two-by-fours, lead pipes, hunks of masonry and concrete. Lester screamed again. The women fell upon him and dragged him down. A woman whose head was a fractured ruin lifted a piece of concrete and smashed Lester's right leg like rotten kindling. Another corpse broke his fingers with a lead pipe.

"Leona," he screamed. "Pleeeease."

Ivy Horse turned her remaining eye toward Leona. The two women faced each other there in the darkness as Lester begged for mercy. One of the dead women jammed a sharpened iron rod into Lester's open mouth and pinned his head to the dirt floor.

Ivy lifted Leona's knife and took a step toward her.

Leona turned and ran up the stairs, through the hall and out into the night. Behind her in the dark, Lester's screams became a babbling shriek.

Leona ran on, toward home, toward freedom. In her left hand she gripped a tiny red and white doll no bigger than her palm.

It sang to her and told her who she was.

BLOODBATH AT LANDSDALE TOWERS

Danny Wahlberg, twenty one, white, and dumb as a box of chicken turds, cleared his throat, blinked three times and said: "You want me to do what?"

Lennox Ravanaugh, thirty-nine, black and mean as a Republican with a rattlesnake up his dickhole, held up one of a dozen little plastic packets that sat on the table in front of him.

"I said I want you to fuck your sister in the ass."

White Bitch - who had once answered to the name Carrie-Ellen Wahlberg - shook her blond head and pulled a knife.

"You stay the fuck away from me, Danny."

Ravanaugh looked back and forth between the twins. They were good for a few more weeks at least. He chuckled and sniffed the little packet.

"Bubble bubble toil and trouble," he said.

The packet held five chunks of rock cocaine. When smoked, they would produce the kind of chemical satisfaction that squirmed its way down into your DNA, checked out the accommodations and said "Make Room For Daddy."

"Weeeelll?" Ravanaugh sang.

Danny glanced over at his sister, who had certainly seen better days.

"Don't even think about it, Danny," White Bitch said. "I'll cut your fucking nuts off."

Danny shook his head and turned back to Ravanaugh.

"I don't think she's gonna go for it, 'Naugh"

Ravanaugh smirked.

"Well that's a shame," he said. "Ain't it, fellas?"

Ravanaugh's Crew, a ragtag motley made up of some of the stupidest humans on Earth, made cattle sounds. Goat, Ravanaugh's best runner, cackled and spat out two of his teeth. The teeth hit the cheap linoleum and bounced under the sofa like a pair of rotten dice. Rook, Lil' Knot and Pabo, Ravanaugh's lieutenants, laughed and threw used condoms at each other.

"Yo Goat," Ravanaugh said.

He flicked the packet over his shoulder.

Goat was nineteen years old and looked sixty, but he scampered across the room with the dexterity that only lifelong junkies can muster and caught the packet before it hit the floor.

"Hell yeah, boss," he panted. "Hell yeah."

Goat produced a pipe and lit up. A sound like a fresh sucking chest wound filled apartment 1654. Then Goat leaned back and closed his eyes.

Danny Wahlberg drooled on his sneakers.

"Sis," he whined.

"No, Danny," White Bitch said. "The hand job was bad enough."

But White Bitch was weakening. She backed up onto the mattress that served as Goat's palette. The mattress smelled like the septic field of a Mexican abortion clinic at high tide. White Bitch's blade dipped. Her attention fluttered between Danny and the Goat.

Ravanaugh heaved a contented sigh.

"Ah, nothing stokes my juices quite like snappin' the moral backbone of upper middle class privilege."

Ravanaugh lived for grinding down the ones from Chicago's Northern suburbs, the ones whose parents sucked ass for Haliburton or Exxon or any of the mega-corps that were corn-holing the planetary working class.

By 2010 raging unemployment, abetted by four successive Bush administrations, had forged a Darwinian nightmare for the residents of the Landsdale Towers Residential Estates. The gauntlet of drug dealers, crack whores and child molesters that stalked the seven mile stretch of State Street that contained the LTRE made life in the projects as pleasant as crawling through the anal tract of a rabid she-moose at the height of mating season.

The college basketball scouts made it worse.

But any guilt Ravanaugh might have felt - since he ran the criminal operations that centered around the Towers - paled beside his outrage at the depredations of Corporate America.

"See, fellas?" Ravanaugh said. "A middle class white kid'll shank his grandmama if you fuck with his sense of entitlement. Observe."

Ravanaugh swept the packets off the tabletop and into the open briefcase on his lap. He snapped the briefcase shut. Danny jumped as if Ravanaugh had fired a shotgun.

"Gimme that briefcase, you cunt," White Bitch snarled. "Or I'll stick this knife up your fat ass."

Lil' Knot and Pabo snickered. Over in the corner, the Goat nodded and fell off of his chair.

"Last chance, Dan," Ravanaugh said. "How 'bout it?"

Danny turned and lurched, zombie-like, toward White Bitch. White Bitch whirled and slashed a long red gash from his inner elbow to his palm. Danny howled.

"Owww!"

He smacked White Bitch across the jaw, knocking the knife across the room. White Bitch swung a booted foot up and caught Danny square in the balls. Danny let out a whoooof, clutched himself and dropped face-first onto the mattress.

"Bravo," Ravanaugh said. Then he picked up a packet and held it out to White Bitch. She reached for it.

"Ah ah ahhh," Ravanaugh whispered.

White Bitch hesitated. Ravanaugh lifted the packet and sniffed it.

"Mmmmmhhh goooood," he said.

White Bitch unzipped her jeans and went over to the mattress. Ravanaugh laughed, his barrel chest filling the room with bad humor.

"We should have brought hay," he said.

"White folks are so fucking depraved."

***

Ravanaugh was just about to make White Bitch blow the whole Crew when someone knocked on the door.

Danny was lying on the mattress with his underpants around his ankles. White Bitch was trying to crawl out from under Mosquito. Mosquito, who was diabetic, had passed out on top of White Bitch while pounding her into a thin paste on the cheap industrial strength carpet. Mosquito weighed nearly four hundred pounds. White Bitch lay spread-eagled beneath a fifth of a ton of insulin resistant mocha man mountain.

Ravanaugh said, "See who it is."

Rook, Ravanaugh's second-in-command, strode over to the door, a Glock nine mm gripped in his fist.

"Who the fuck is it?" Rook shouted.

"A better question might be: Who the heck are you?"

Ravanaugh and Crew spun around.

A black man wearing a long, camel-brown duster and a white ten gallon hat was standing in the doorway to the bedroom.

"Who the fuck are you?" Ravanaugh said. "How the fuck did you get in here?"

Duster shook his head.

"Mister, you sure got a dirty mouth."

Ravanaugh stared at the stranger. He appeared middle aged and stood about six-two, maybe six-three. His chest and shoulders were broad, his middle free of anything resembling fat. Duster looked like the sort of man who got his exercise ripping boulders out of the earth with his bare hands.

The Crew drew down. Duster didn't seem to notice.

"What's with that fucked up outfit?" Ravanaugh said.

Duster made a tsking sound.

"Anybody ever tell you fellas it ain't polite to say the F-word s'much?" he said. "'Specially in the presence of a lady?"

"What lady...?" Ravanaugh said.

Duster nodded toward the front door. The woman standing in the doorway might not have been Eartha Kitt's younger, hotter sister but she surely could have passed for her.

"Hello boys."

She was wearing a red leather catsuit.

85

Red stiletto heels put the woman at about six feet two inches tall. She was the color of milk chocolate; her short black hair combed backward and slicked down. She had the blackest eyes Ravanaugh had ever seen.

Ravanaugh's eyes darted back and forth between the invaders like a man watching someone play tennis with his balls.

"Who are you people?" he said.

Duster stepped forward and took his hat off.

"My name is Nathaniel Corners. That over there's my associate, Miss Negrita Marcos."

"Negrita?" Pabo said. "Que tu quiere, mama?"

Negrita bowed smoothly from the hips and answered him in Spanish. Her voice was heavy, dusky, like her skin.

"She said they come a long way to meet you, boss," Pabo said.

Negrita smiled. Her teeth were very, very white.

"You are Lenny Ravanaugh," Corners said. "But on the street they call you Highball."

"Lenny," Lil' Knot snorted. Corners laughed. Ravanaugh's gut tightened and his mouth went dry. That's not a man standing there, he thought. Nothing like a man and you know it, don't you?

"Hey, Ravanaugh. What's happenin'?"

Ravanaugh turned to see Danny rising to his feet. The male twin looked like he'd been drinking cat piss in a fallout shelter for the last three months.

"Who the fuck is this clown?" he said.

Corners stopped chuckling. His smile winked out of existence: There was no gradual relaxing of facial muscles. It was simply there one moment and gone the next.

86

"I don't cotton to that kind of talk," Corners said.

Danny shrugged and pulled up his shorts.

"Let me gank this asshole, Naugh," Rook said.

He lifted his Glock and aimed it at Corners. Lil' Knot and Pabo followed suit.

"Chill," Ravanaugh said. "Let's hear the man out."

"Yo, this is bullshit," Danny said. I don't have to listen to this asshole."

Corners turned toward Danny and said: "You call me outta my name one more time, sonny-jim, and you're gonna call down the thunder."

Danny lifted his middle finger. "Fuck. You. *Asshole.*"

"Wait..." Ravanaugh said.

Corners' right arm moved. Something flicked past Ravanaugh's left ear. Then Danny's hands flew up and fluttered against his face like startled doves.

"Get it off get it off get off me!" he screamed.

Blood splashed down the fronts of Danny's arms, streaked his white skin with slashes of red; gouts of flesh flew from between his clenched fists. He screamed and fell to the floor.

"What's happening?" White Bitch squeaked. "Danny?"

Danny arched and bucked on the floor, his head and heels drumming on bare cement where the linoleum had worn through. Then he lay still. A single robin's egg blue eye glared at Ravanaugh through a mask of blood. The other half of Danny's face was a gaping red crater.

"Son of a bitch," Rook whispered.

Then something climbed out of Danny's eye socket. It was the size and shape of a hockey puck. A dozen black spider's legs extended out of the thing. It rose up on those perfect black legs, skittered up Danny's forehead and settled on the crown of his skull.

Two legs scooped out a chunk of Danny's eye socket and smeared it into a pink slit along the top of the hockey puck. Ravanaugh saw a tiny black tongue slide out of the slit and lap up the red glob.

"Bullshit," Ravanaugh said.

Pabo and Lil' Knot scrambled past the woman in red and fled down the hallway. Rook lifted his Glock.

Negrita moved. Ravanaugh was still staring at the empty doorway before he realized she was gone. He spun; Negrita was standing behind Rook. She grabbed his right arm and wrenched it up behind his back. Then she grabbed him by the scruff of the neck, bent him forward and yanked his arm over his head, lifting him up onto his toes.

"Let me go, you crazy bitch!" Rook said.

"Oooh," Negrita purred. "Talk dirty to me, pusher man."

Then she broke his arm. Crack! And Rook screamed and dropped his gun.

Negrita drew back her fist and punched Rook in the back of the head. The front of his face pooched outward from the blow. Hydrostatic pressure did the rest. Rook's forehead exploded and spattered the floor with thirty-five years' worth of bad news.

"Danny?" White Bitch screamed. "I can't breathe!"

Over in the corner, Mosquito had slipped into a diabetic coma. White Bitch was stuck.

Corners seemed intent on enjoying Negrita's display. His laughter sliced the air like ravens' wings.

"Now that's what I call black comedy," he said. "Wouldn't you agree, Ravanaugh?"

Lil' Knot and Pabo were gone, but Ravanaugh knew they would have to pass two dozen killers on their way down to the street. He congratulated himself on having had the foresight to murder all the local gang leaders; it had made hiring their homeboys that much simpler. Ravanaugh could almost hear his kill squad thundering toward them. *Money well spent,* he thought. *Any second now.*

Even with Death staring him in the face, Ravanaugh remained a businessman. Life and Death were his business and there was always another angle to exploit.

"What's next?" he said.

Corners turned, one eyebrow raised.

"How's that?"

Ravanaugh shrugged.

"Since I'm still suckin' wind I figure y'all must want something. Let's conversate."

Negrita draped her arm across his shoulders.

"We want information," she said.

Ravanaugh's nose crinkled. Negrita smelled of perfume, something fruity, like the stuff his more upscale call girls used before meeting a date. Beneath the perfume however, lurked another smell, something that reminded Ravanaugh of fresh roadkill on a hot summer day.

"What kind of - of information?" he said.

Corners strode over to where Goat lay unconscious on the floor. He bent down, his brow furrowed, and shook his head. Then he whistled.

The hockey puck that killed Danny Wahlberg rolled across the floor, leaving a trail of blood. The Death Puck stopped at Goat's high top sneakers. Then it climbed up Corners' leg and disappeared into his pocket.

Corners bent over and examined the Goat. He pulled a Smith & Wesson Model 19 Combat Magnum out of a holster on his left hip, thumbed back the hammer, and placed the barrel against Goat's forehead. "This one's done," he said. Then he pulled the trigger. The blast drowned out Ravanaugh's roar of outrage.

"Names," Corners said.

"You're crazy, motherfucker!"

"Ah ah ah," Negrita said. "Profanity is the last refuge of the weak-minded."

"Fuck you, bitch!"

Corners stepped over Goat's body.

"I warned you," he said.

Then he ripped Ravanaugh's ear off.

Ravanaugh screamed; blood jumped out of his head and spattered the right shoulder of his new Armani running suit. He fell to his knees, stomach heaving as bile burned a fireline up the back of his throat. *Help me,* he thought. *Where are they?*

Negrita picked up his ear and pocketed it. Then she slid a long-bladed dagger from a sheath on her ankle and started doing things to the three corpses. Ravanaugh gagged.

Corners leaned down and spoke softly.

"Let me make it plain for you, sonny-jim," he said.

He grabbed Ravanaugh's right wrist, raised his hand to eye level and grabbed his index finger.

"You will provide the names and phone numbers of every dealer, every runner, every contact you currently employ."

Ravanaugh's eyes widened.

"You must be outta your goddamned..."

POP

Ravanaugh snarled and bit back his scream. Corners released the finger he'd broken and grabbed its neighbor.

"You will provide this information, or I'll call Nat Jr. out to play, and believe me, Nat Jr.'s gonna do more than pop a few knuckles, right son?"

The Death puck climbed up onto Corners' shoulder and shrieked. Nat Jr. sounded like a monkey with a throat full of razor blades. Something warm and wet landed on Ravanaugh's forehead and settled over his left eye. Half blind, Ravanaugh broke.

"Please," he said. "Get it off me."

"Nat Jr. likes you," Corners said. "Findin' the right playmate for your pups is so important these days."

Nat Jr. stroked Ravanaugh's left eyelid with one of his legs. Ravanaugh began to cry.

"In - in my briefcase," he said. "My - my phone. It's got all the names and numbers on it."

Negrita retrieved the briefcase and opened it. Inside lay twelve thousand dollars worth of powder and rock cocaine, along with two handguns and three wireless phones.

"Easy peezy," Negrita said.

She put the items she'd harvested from the two dead men, along with Ravanaugh's ear, in the briefcase. Danny's blue eyeball winked at Ravanaugh before Negrita shut the lid.

"Witch's brew," she hummed.

Ravanaugh looked up at Corners.

"P - please don't kill me."

"Alright," Corners said.

He stepped back. Then Negrita yanked Ravanaugh's head back and sliced his jugular. Ravanaugh clutched at his throat, trying to staunch the blood gushing between his fingers.

"Somebody...help..." he sputtered.

Then he dropped.

The strangers stood in the center of the room with their eyes closed. Outside, a passing pigeon blew apart in a Technicolor burp-blast of blood and feathers.

Corners moved first.

"Okay then," he said.

Negrita said, "Had enough?"

Nat Jr. shrieked, curled itself into a ball and slipped back into Corners' pocket.

"Not quite done," Corners said. "But we should move on."

Corners strode out into the hallway and headed toward the elevator. Negrita hefted the briefcase, but a flicker of motion caught her eye. She whirled, knife in hand.

A smile lit up Negrita's supermodel face.

"Oh ho," she grinned. "What have we here?"

The woman in red glided across the room to where White Bitch peered out from beneath her fleshy prison.

Negrita chuckled. "You look like you're wearing a babushka made out of chocolate- covered chitlin's."

She kicked Mosquito in the ribs. Her boot disappeared up to the ankle in a gelatinous fold near his armpit.

"What...the...hell?" Mosquito grunted.

Negrita leaned down and sniffed.

"Diabetic," she said. "Asshole."

Then she jammed her knife into Mosquito's right ear. Mosquito shuddered and vomited all over White Bitch. Negrita grimaced and rolled him off of the girl.

"Hello, treasure," she said. "What's your name?"

"White..." White Bitch shook her head and cleared her throat, "I mean...Carrie-Ellen Wahlberg, ma'am."

Negrita stooped and helped Carrie-Ellen stand up.

"Let's get you out of here, honey," she said.

"My - my brother," Carrie-Ellen said.

"Dead, I'm afraid," Negrita said, "Best not to look."

Carrie-Ellen accepted the bad news as gracefully as a woman wearing a body fluid cocktail dress can.

"Fuck this," she said.

"Language, dear," Negrita said.

Corners was waiting at the elevator.

"Look what I found, partner," Negrita sang.

Corners smiled. The elevator doors slid open.

"Whoa," Corners said.

The shaft was empty. No elevator waited beyond the doors. Arnold Schwarzenegger's Terminator glared at Corners, emblazoned in silver and red on the back wall of the shaft. A lightless abyss stretched away beneath his feet.

"Pity the children," Corners said.

A volley of curses erupted from apartment 1646.

"Better hurry," Negrita said.

"What are we gonna do?" Carrie-Ellen said.

Corners extended his right hand.

"Trust me, baby doll?"

Carrie-Ellen nodded. She placed her small pink hand in Corners' big brown one. Then Corners whipped her around and threw her into the elevator shaft. Carrie-Ellen bounced off the back wall and fell screaming into the darkness.

"Now I'm done," Corners said.

From around the corner, the sounds of a posse filled the hallway. Corners extended his left hand.

"Shall we, milady?"

Negrita gripped the briefcase in her left hand and gave Corners her right. Together, they stepped into the elevator shaft and went up, Corners' duster flapping behind him like wings in the darkness.

They held hands as they rose.

DORMANT

White noise filled Hopkins' head.

Twenty-four hours.

"Mr. Hopkins? Can you hear me?"

Twenty-four hours to live.

Hopkins shook the white noise out of his head.

"What did you say?" he said.

The doctor, a young Pakistani with long eyelashes, nodded with practiced sympathy, as if he'd delivered the same report too many times to count.

"The organism inside your body is commonly known as an extraterrestrial bipedatropic micro-carnivore; EBM for short. You've seen the recent headlines?"

Hopkins nodded. Who hadn't seen the ghastly images? Millions of human beings, their bodies writhing as the 'space worms' gnawed through their hosts' bowels.

"I read somewhere that some hosts have been able to stun the worms using hypersonics," Hopkins said.

"Ahh yes," the doctor said. "Hypersonics have proven effective in crippling the EBM's sensory apparatus: the fine network of tentacles located at both ends of the organism. The worm dies and can be removed from the intestinal tract by a simple surgical procedure."

"Yes!" Hopkins shouted.

The doctor flashed his sympathetic smile again.

"However, I'm afraid Accounting has informed me that you simply cannot afford the treatment."

Hopkins sat, stunned. The doctor glanced at his watch.

"There are a number of excellent pain relievers on the black market, Mr. Hopkins," he said. "I'd recommend that you secure one. I would do it very quickly."

Outside, a city bus lay on its side in the center of the intersection. As Hopkins emerged from the clinic he saw a crowd of people clustered around the front end. Through the swaying forest of bodies, Hopkins could see a man writhing on the cement.

The writhing man was tall and blonde, wearing a tie-dyed t-shirt, khaki shorts and sandals: probably one of the wealthy European tourists who haunted Times Square searching for cheap meta-drugs.

Someone in the crowd screamed, and the watchers broke apart like minnows fleeing a Tiger Shark. The European twisted in a spreading pool of blood as his worm chewed its way out. The EBM had become disoriented. One end had eaten through most of the European's lower face; squirming black proboscis whipped and wriggled where the European's mouth nose and eyes should have been.

The worm opened the mouth at its anterior end and uttered a gibbering metallic shriek. It bared a gleaming mouthful of razor sharp teeth and wrapped its blind head around the front bumper of the bus, struggling to pull itself from its host, even as the posterior end pushed its way out of the European's anus. It shrieked as it thrashed, twisting in a gush of red/brown matter as the European's head and heels drummed against the hot concrete.

Hopkins turned away from the crowd and began to walk. He chose no particular direction. At his first sight of the European's worm the EBM in his guts had begun to squirm. Hopkins walked. But as the twisting ache began in his stomach, he began to run.

THE UGLY TRUTH

"I can't tell who's uglier, the man or the pig."

Molo Kananda glanced up at the tall, mahogany skinned noblewoman. Her white even teeth bared in a snarl of distaste. She shone in the crimson glow of the setting sun. With the gold that encircled her long neck, she could have bought Molo outright.

A servant whisked the tall woman away and escorted her into the great silken wedding pavilion. Molo laid his hand on Juba's massive flank.

"Easy, boy," he crooned. "Easy."

Molo Kananda came from a long line of ugly people. No one even remotely pleasant looking had ever allowed a single molecule of DNA to come near Molo's unlovely ancestors.

This genetic social deathblow had become painfully obvious when upon Molo's birth, his own mother flung up her hands and cried, "Pluck out mine eyes! Seal up my womb for all eternity! Spay me lest I bring forth monsters!"

It was said - mostly by the old men who drink berry wine in the *Shanzi* Lodges of Ghoval after long days of running antelope and fighting werepanthers - that Molo Pigsplitter had "fallen face first out of the world's tallest Ugly Tree and struck every branch on the way down."

But Molo had no way of knowing these things. He'd inherited the nickname 'Pigsplitter' through no fault of his own; having been abandoned, still steaming from his mother's womb, upon the doorstep of the *Goa*. When the strangely quiet newborn had been brought before Master Kani, the *bladeseer* of Ghoval's mysterious school for bladed combat, the headmaster had studied his features intently. Affixed to the infant's blanket was a note bearing a simple message: *Ward this child as I cannot. He bears a gift more precious than beauty.*

The signature adorning the letter belonged to Dogen Maseni, the greatest sorcerer in all of Unan.

When Master Kani dispatched runners to Maseni's palace at the northern end of Ghoval, however, they'd found it abandoned, with no sign that it had ever been the home of the nation's mightiest mage.

Dogen Maseni was never seen again.

Molo was the son of N'tosi, Maseni's housekeeper; a woman whose personal unattractiveness had once stopped a rampaging rhinophant dead in its tracks. Some whispered that Dogen Maseni (who had shattered more than a few mirrors himself) had fathered Molo on N'tosi before departing the mortal world for realms unknown. The truth, alas, was never known. N'tosi (whose name in the High Speech of Ghoval translates roughly as 'Near-sighted Dung Bride') died days after Molo's birth.

Noting the infant's protruding brow and yielding chin (a sure sign of ignoble lineage in the beauty obsessed culture of Unan's capitol city) Master Kani had given him into the care of the *sook i-makopu:* the pig tenders of the *Goa.*

Molo had grown up learning the ways of the giant wild pigs that terrorized the mountainous regions of Ghoval, under the stewardship of old Dapu U'wambe. U'wambe had proven a kind enough father; he only beat Molo until Molo was big enough to hit back. But he'd taught Molo how to wrestle an unruly *makopu* to the ground, the surest methods for capturing the beasts without damaging their meat, and, most importantly, the slaughtering rites which hallowed the animal's flesh while simultaneously honoring Cero-U, the war god who presided over the Hamado, the Three Hundred Gods of Unan.

It was an ancient tradition therefore, for high-ranking members of the *Goa* to offer a hallowed *makopu* at important ceremonies.

None was more important than this.

"On this day we honor the Princess M'kele M'butu N'tozake Letitia Molumbo," the Royal *Jaba* cried loudly from inside the wedding tent.

Molo stood up and cracked his knuckles.

"On this day, She Whom the Gods Bless in Grace and Beauty to Confound the Sun, Moon and Stars orders her Consorts, who number among the greatest swordsmen in Unan!"

"Aren't you coming?"

Molo smiled and turned toward the familiar voice.

It was Milane.

Molo didn't know to whom she belonged or where she worked. All he knew was that the plain faced servant girl had visited him nearly every day of that year.

At first her visits had irritated him. She enjoyed challenging him with questions, riddles that left him perturbed and irritated for hours after her departure. In time, her unquenchable curiosity, combined with her subversive wit appealed to him. He came to look forward to their visits.

"I'm busy," he said with mock gruffness. "Go away."

Milane leaned over the fence that surrounded the makeshift pen. The twinkle in her eye informed him that she wasn't finished with him yet.

"Surely all the Great and Beautiful of Ghoval will attend such an important performance," she said.

Molo shrugged.

"I am neither."

Milane smiled.

"That makes two of us."

Her smile dimmed. She stooped, plucked a smooth stone from the dirt and considered its shape.

"Have you ever dreamed of a different kind of life, Molo Kananda?" she said quietly. Molo studied her for a moment. Then he shrugged.

"There is only one life."

This seemed to stir something in the servant girl. Her clear brown eyes glittered as she stared into the distance.

"What's wrong with you?" Molo said.

A hunting horn sounded from the wedding tent. Milane flung the smooth stone across the pen and climbed down from the fence.

"I have to go," she said, "Goodbye Molo."

"Wait," Molo called. "Milane?"

But she was gone.

Molo gestured toward the slaughtering trough where he would end the *makopu's* life. The boar rubbed its whiskers against his cheek, turned and trotted over to the trough.

Molo sighed as U'wambe's voice rose up in his memory.

"The magician was right, boy," U'wambe had said. "You possess a most dangerous gift; the capacity... to *understand*."

Molo shook his head. One thing he was certain he *didn't* understand was Milane and every other member of her sex. But U'wambe was right about his other talents. Molo possessed a certain understanding of the great carnivorous pigs. Five years earlier, with sixteen summers behind him, he'd discovered this gift after a saber-tusked, blood-maddened boar had trampled his steward, Dapu U'wambe.

Molo was working at the far side of the *Goa's* slaughtering pen when, alerted by U'wambe's scream of pain, he turned and saw the boar run the old tender down. Molo had grabbed his *sekh*, the long-bladed killing knife used by the pig tenders. As his hand closed around its hilt, the *makopu* turned, roared and charged him.

Molo had sensed the creature's rage. Its blind instinct for destruction and confusion beat at his mind like the thunder of war drums. He'd stood, stunned by the clarity of the makopu's plight. That understanding demanded a response.

Molo began to dance.

It wasn't the sort of dancing that Shenzi O'watu, Ghoval's imperious Royal Dance Minister would have enjoyed; but it was dancing nonetheless.

The boar stopped.

Shaking its massive head like a bull beset by stinging flies, the boar pawed at the dirt and bellowed a challenge. A moment later, the *makopu* had reared up on its stunted hind legs and begun to dance as well.

The two of them had drawn a large crowd before they finished; Molo leaping, pawing the ground and snorting, the *makopu* matching him move for move.

Then Molo had made the mistake of turning his back on the *makopu*, breaking the spell. The boar wheeled and thundered back toward U'wambe.

Molo had sprinted after it, his legs pumping, made strong by a lifetime of chasing the great beasts, and flung himself into its path. The boar had tasted blood and would not stop until it had drained U'wambe's corpse.

Molo had swung his *sekh* - its broad steel blade flashing in the morning sun - and split the boar's skull.

As U'wambe lay dying, he'd spoken the doom of Molo's life.

"You *are* gifted, boy," he'd said, "because you *understand.*"

Remembering his dying master, Molo grabbed his sekh and walked toward the ceremonial trough. Then someone screamed inside the wedding tent.

Molo froze. A roar – as of many voices raised in horror - went up from the crowd inside the silken pavilion. Molo ran toward the tent just as a large group of panicked wedding guests stampeded *out* of it. He spun - his body twisting to avoid trampling - and ducked in through the bright yellow flaps.

Inside, the wedding tent looked like Satan's own slaughterhouse.

Normally, a female of Royal station selected her three Consorts, one from each of the main schools of the Goa. During the Ordering ceremony the chosen three would spar with blades, skill and wits until a marital pecking order had been established.

Master Kani, who was officiating at the ceremony, stood atop the wedding dais beside Queen Omune. King Ra-suldor, a former Consort himself and M'kele's sire, stood protectively in front of them. Molo reflexively glanced away before catching himself. The Royal Family's faces were unveiled. He could see the terror in their eyes.

Princess M'kele stood between Ra-suldor and Master Kani, her face shorn of the familial veil that all of noble birth wore to shield their beauty from the hungry masses. Their eyes met and Molo's world turned on its ear. Disoriented, he staggered backward and sat down on his rump.

The members of the King's Shield lay in a circle around the Royal Family. The guardsmen had been beaten into unrecognizable lumps of blood and bone. Only the three 'Consorts' stood fast, their weapons leveled at the intruder.

A giant corpse loomed in the center of the room.

"Zuvembie!" someone screamed.

The remaining guests fell over themselves to avoid the zombie's crimson stare. The eyes of the undead held the power to steal human souls; enslaving them to the will of whatever dark master they served.

Molo recognized the undead giant and nearly screamed himself.

People in Ghoval still whispered about Koto the Gorefisted and his infamous 'Rain of Blood.' As the Governor of Nantan, Ghoval's neighbor to the north, Koto's solved a month long gang war by dismembering all suspected gang members along with their families and flinging their remains from the walls of the Governor's Palace; while his personal orchestra played the Ghovalese National Anthem.

Molo shuddered. When a zuvembie was created from the body and soul of a violent man, the result was an evil magnified ten-fold.

The three Royal Consorts crouched and moved into an attack formation. Each was skilled in one of the three principal martial arts of the *Goa* school. Each had been raised by Masters. As

Consorts, they were far more than well bred fops; they were trained to be the last line of defense for Princess M'Kele.

Consort Leng leapt toward Koto Gorefist. A Master of *Den Soma*, the Slicing Hand, Leng swept a disarming strike toward Koto's forearm, intending to sever it. A moment later, Leng screamed. Blood spouted from the stump where his muscular right arm had been.

The ambassador from Senea, the City of Stone and Sand, uttered a squawk and soiled his rainbow robes of state.

Leng was officious and cruel. He'd once beaten Molo for daring to watch him during one of his many practice bouts. Leng's skill, however, was beyond dispute. Molo had watched him cut through iron bars with his bare hands. Now Leng's right arm lay in a reservoir of blood at his feet; fingernails scratching convulsively at the floor.

Molo was dimly aware of shouting.

"Protect the Princess!"

"Protect M'kele!"

Consort Cavalu and Consort Makai moved toward the giant zuvembie.

"Don't touch him!"

Master Kani's stentorian warning penetrated Molo's shock. The remaining guests had retreated to the furthest edges of the wedding tent, eager for bloodshed; too afraid to intervene.

Consort Cavalu spun toward the dead giant. He was a Master of *Sedo* - the Killing Dance. Molo had studied Cavalu intently, when his labors were done and he could sneak into the *Sedo* sessions unchallenged. Cavalu was arguably the most powerful of Master Kani's students. Molo had seen him incapacitate as many as five opponents using only his hands and feet and the fist and boot daggers of the *Sedo* discipline.

Cavalu dipped and whirled; his perfect features blurred until Molo could barely distinguish them. The shining daggers of the *Sedo* Master flashed toward Koto, forming a shimmering barrier between The Royal Family and the zombie. Cavalu's skill was so great that even the undead Koto Gorefist took two steps backward.

"*Hold*," Master Kani snapped. Cavalu stopped spinning.

"*Moren'e tuo'c, Koto sevanesu!*" Master Kani cried.

The zombie turned, its nostrils flaring as if it scented some dark delicacy in the air.

Master Kani lifted his double bladed *stave*, the ceremonial weapon of the bladeseer. A white flare of power leapt from the stave and struck Koto D'umbualleh with the rumble of an erupting volcano.

Koto tottered; the crimson fire flashed in his eyes. Then he fell to his knees, threw back his head and burst into flames.

Cavalu pressed the attack, sped forward to cut the heart from the zuvembie's breast: Other than beheading, it was the only known non-magical way to destroy the undead.

Master Kani's shout rang out over the din.

"Hold! Fool! Have you no eyes in that pretty head?"

Cavalu stopped, his blades a tiger's whisker from Koto's chest.

"Why do you forbid, Master?" Cavalu grated.

"Typical Consort," Master Kani said. "Loaded between the legs, *empty* between the ears."

Master Kani spat on the floor. He glanced at Molo as if it were the most natural thing in the world for the pig tender to be standing in the same tent with Ghovalese nobility.

"Explain what has happened to this *love toy*," he snarled, gesturing toward Consort Leng. Molo studied the unmoving zuvembie with the special dimension of his perceptions. Then he nodded and spoke.

"The zuvembie is both a weapon and a trap," he said.

"Whatever force is used against Koto Gorefist will rebound upon its wielder tenfold."

The Consorts scowled.

Master Kani nodded his vulture-like head with something like vindication.

"You dishonor us, Master," Cavalu muttered. "To favor this gawking swill drinker over your chosen students."

"Oh, be silent," Master Kani hissed. "He *understands*."

"Understands what?" Consort Makai sneered.

"What is needed most," Master Kani snapped.

The old bladeseer crept forward, his stave held before him like the wand of a blind water smeller, toward the burning zombie, who appeared to have lost the power of movement.

"This is a magical foe, my pretty idiots," he said. "Not one to be dispatched like a common thug."

Master Kani made an arcane gesture and extinguished the flames. Cavalu and Makai bowed, chastened.

Master Kani sniffed at the black smoke that drifted up from the zuvembie. Then he spat on the teak wood floor.

"Pah," he snarled. "This one has been cursed by a *bomwodesu*, a necromancer."

The wedding guests gasped. Some mouthed words of warding to repel evil spirits attracted to Master Kani's fell utterance.

"Koto D'umbualleh has been resurrected and sent to disrupt this ceremony."

"But why?" Cavalu rumbled, "Who would create such an abomination?"

"Oh, a few assholes leap to mind," Master Kani said. "But I will glean the truth, with your permission, my King."

Ra-suldor nodded. He grasped M'kele to his breast and nodded assurance at Queen Omune.

Master Kani approached the zombie, who knelt on the floor with ropes of sizzling green drool drizzling out of its mouth. Then he raised his stave and rapped Koto across the forehead.

There was a white flash. A smell like lightning over deep water filled the pavilion. When Molo could see again, Master Kani was lying on his back and the zombie was lying on its face.

Molo shrugged through the Consorts and hurried to Master Kani's side. The bladeseer was already sitting up, mumbling to himself. Occasionally he would flail about with his stave trying to hit one of the Junior Flower Girls.

"See," Ra-suldor said. "Koto Gorefist has been defiled in more ways than one."

The King pointed to a long slit that extended from between Koto's buttocks to the base of his neck. Molo saw what looked like hundreds of rough stitches sewn along the length of the slit.

"Looks like he's been stitched together," Molo said.

"Yes, but by whom?" Ra-suldor said. "And for what purpose?"

111

Suddenly, a sound like meat sizzling over a cooking fire filled the wedding tent. A torrent of black smoke belched out of the incision in Koto's back.

"Get back!" Molo said.

A fist punched through the smoldering rend. Then a head, followed by powerful shoulders, emerged through the slit. It was a man, or something that looked like a man, its body corded with muscle, stocky and thick-wristed as a Senean twelve year old. Its skin was pale as rotted milk. Its lips protruded over a mouth of sharp, yellow teeth.

The top half of the creature's face was devoid of feature. Above its wide baboon's nose two black holes gaped where its eyes should have been. It was one of the *su'pasha,* the pitiless race of assassins that inhabited the Crimson City, far to the North.

And it was unmistakably dead.

"I have drawn offense from the Royal House of Ra-suldor," the creature rasped in an imperious tone that even Master Kani would have been hard-pressed to match. The remaining wedding guests gasped. The voice that issued from the *su'pasha's* mouth had terrorized the people of Unan for centuries.

"Nemeha Juvisee, protect us," Ra-suldor swore. "Why do you darken this holy day, Samael Corpse Eater?"

Six wedding goers fainted. The Ambassador from Senea, awakened only moments earlier, screamed and fainted again.

"Just the asshole I suspected!" Master Kani cried triumphantly.

With that, the bladeseer fell flat on his face.

The pale creature turned toward Ra-suldor.

"I petitioned thee for thy daughter's hand in marriage and you rudely denied me." it said. "I offer a final chance, Ra-suldor Suldor-son. Wilt thou grant me thy daughter?"

"No, father!" M'kele cried. "I cannot love such a thing as this!"

Ra-suldor took a step toward the su'pasha.

"To my daughter's refusal, I add my own," he said.

"Leave this place, Samael, or risk the damnation of the Holy Three Hundred."

The *su'pasha* seemed to consider for a moment. It cocked its blind head to the left as if listening to the tolling of a distant bell. Then it laughed.

"I was damned centuries before you were born, *fool*," it said in Samael's voice. "Tonight, however, I will repent my damnation while I luxuriate in thy daughter's blood."

Molo drew his *sekh*. "Ware!" he cried, too late. A moment later, the Royal Consorts thrust him aside.

"Lie there, where you belong, pigsplitter," Cavalu spat. "This conflict is beyond you."

The *su'pasha* leapt high over the heads of the Consorts and landed next to Ra-suldor and M'kele. Moving in unison, the Consorts brandished their blades. Consort Makai had mastered the assassin's art of *Valakata*, the Unseen Saber. He feinted toward the pale creature and vanished.

The *su'pasha* made a short slashing gesture. Somewhere in the distance, came a sound like a rumble of thunder beneath the Earth. A moment later, the pale creature gripped a scimitar in each fist.

113

Whirling, the su'pasha assassin thrust one blade over its head. The sound of clashing steel rang out and sparks flew from its upraised blade. Molo could see no attacker. Consort Makai was a true *Valakatan* Adept.

The assassin parried a blow from Cavalu, who had spun to attack its flank, then it launched a left-handed attack upon the clear air directly to its left. More sparks flew, and Molo thought he heard Makai grunt in surprise or pain.

Cavalu spun in, Sedo blades slashing, and scored the *su'pasha* across the backs of its legs, shoulders and head. Blood splashed the floor of the wedding tent. But Cavalu was too close. Sensing an opening, the su'pasha lunged and beheaded the powerful Consort with one scimitar while fending off Makai with the other.

Cavalu's beautiful head whirled past Molo and bounced out of the wedding pavilion.

Molo leaped to his feet.

The *su'pasha* hammered at its invisible opponent, smashing sparks from the empty air until there came a sound like a curse spat by Onu the God of tainted steel. It was the sound of a saber breaking.

Makai materialized, bloody and battered, on his knees before the grinning *su'pasha*. A moment later, his head joined Cavalu's in the dust.

The assassin turned toward the Royal Family.

Molo Kananda barred the way, his sekh raised on high.

"What manner of working- class insolence be this?" Samael snorted. "What do you want, pig tender?"

Molo ignored the taunt; he'd endured much worse in the pens of the *Goa*. He lifted his head and spoke clearly.

"I am your doom, Eater of dead flesh."

Samael scowled, squinting eyelessly, as if Molo were too small to see clearly. Then he laughed. The sound of the *bomwodesu's* contempt sucked the air from the room; its force made Molo's ears bleed.

"You would challenge me for her?" he said. "Then you will suffer the fate of all who fight for love."

It was true. Molo *had* fallen in love. And though he knew he could never hope to claim the

115

Princess for himself, neither would he countenance her destruction at the hands of Samael Corpse-eater.

Samael, in the flesh of the *su'pasha,* whirled his scimitars and attacked.

Molo vanished.

A startled gasp rose from the wedding goers. Even the *su'pasha* halted, snapping its head about in sudden confusion.

Molo reappeared *behind* the assassin, reversed his grip on his *sekh* and launched a hammer blow which struck the back of the *su'pasha's* skull with enough force to send the pale creature sprawling.

Molo flipped the *sekh,* grasped its hilt and advanced on the assassin. But Samael was prepared for him. As Molo approached, the *su'pasha* sprang to its feet. The scimitars disappeared as if they'd been absorbed into the assassin's skin, and a spiked silver ball and chain appeared between its fists.

The *su'pasha* whirled the melon sized ball like a fisherman hunting trout with a *bolo* net. He flung it toward Molo. The power of the silver ball fried the air as it screamed toward the pig tender's head.

Molo became a whirring blur of motion; He spun out of the way as the silver ball struck the wooden floor, splintering it.

The *su'pasha* struggled to free the weapon; Molo whirled across the room - blade flashing like the claws of a *Houngasi* sand devil - and slashed its throat; once, twice, thrice. Cuts and gouges appeared as if by magic in the *su'pasha's* flesh. Blood flew from Molo's blade, a shining red pinwheel spewing crimson droplets around the tent.

Molo stopped spinning. The *su'pasha* roared and thundered toward him.

Molo cartwheeled easily out of its path. But at the last instant, the assassin grabbed one of his legs, swung him around in a wide circle and released him. Molo flew across the wedding tent, crashed into the main support pillar, bounced off and landed on the marble wedding dais.

The Royal Family scattered.

The *su'pasha* leapt onto the wedding dais and swept Molo up in its claws.

"Now, pigsplitter," Samael snarled. "Learn the price of your devotion."

From the scarred flesh of its forearm, the *su'pasha* withdrew a long, curved dagger and pressed its edge to Molo's throat. Then it screamed.

Molo blinked the shadows from his eyes.

Princess M'kele stood behind the *su'pasha*, her brown fists clenched around Master Kani's ceremonial stave. The other end was buried in the top of the *su'pasha's* skull.

The su'pasha lashed out with one massive arm and knocked M'kele from the wedding dais.

Molo summoned the last dregs of his energy, flattened his right hand, stiffening his fingers until his joints ached. He had studied Consort Leng, observed his mastery of the Slicing Hand until his mind ached. Steeling himself, he summoned his power and struck. His fingers sheared through the meat of the *su'pasha's* throat, passed through the creature's spinal column, and out the back of its neck.

The *su'pasha's* head fell from its shoulders, struck the dais and bounced across the floor of the wedding tent.

Nothing moved.

Molo drifted for a while upon a sea of pain and exhaustion. But finally, someone grabbed his hand and tugged him gently toward the shore of awakening. He opened his eyes and looked up into the face of the servant girl who visited him every day.

"Milane."

The Princess smiled, pride and wit sparkling like joy in her eyes. Her plain features lit Molo's dark places like the light from a warm summer sun: She was the most beautiful woman in Ghoval.

And she had always been his friend.

"Have you ever dreamed of another kind of life, Molo Kananda?" she whispered through tears.

Molo smiled back.

He understood her perfectly.

THE LONG, LOST LIFE OF RUFUS BLEAK

This time it's the scent of pine that brings him back. He even recognizes the brand: Pine-All; for that deep forest clean. If he still believed in Daddy's Hell, Rufus Bleak would pray for damnation.

Different...kinds of...Hell, Bleak thinks.

He has to squint to make out the nearest features in a room he doesn't recognize. A digital alarm holo chimes three feet away, but Bleak can't discern more than a green glow. He turns his head to the left, toward the pool of sunlight warming his pillow and feels wetness on his cheek. His new host is drooling.

He turns back; a vague outline of a woman in white stands at the side of his bed.

"Rise and shine, Kenny," the figure says.

"Loretta's here. Time for potty."

Why do they always use pine? Bleak thinks. As if scented chemicals could scrub away the truth of this place.

'Sit up,' he tells the new body.

Nothing happens.

Move the right hand, he thinks. *The left?*

Loretta grabs him under the arms, yanks him out of bed and hauls him across the room. She is bigger than Bleak in this body and she smells like milk. For a moment, the artificial pine fades.

Sour, Bleak thinks. *Like Sister Rebecca.*

The sternest member of his lost congregation, Sister Rebecca revived those Brothers and Sisters in Christ who succumbed to the Arkansas heat and their self-induced passions during his sermons. At the height of his powers Bleak could bring the whole congregation thundering to its feet, rocking the chapel with cries of "Hallelujah!" and "Preach, Reverend!"

"Oh, for Pete's piss," the woman says. "Loretta forgot your glasses. You're as blind as a bat aren't you, Kenny?"

Bleak feels her slip something over his nose, and the world jumps into focus.

A hospice.

He can see a row of beds lining the walls in front and behind him. The other beds contain men, many of them old, twisted; a rogue's gallery of the squawking half-dead.

Some kind of convalescent home.

"I'm short on chairs, Kenny," Loretta whispers into his ear. "Gonna get my tai-bo, haulin' you boys around today."

Bleak hears several residents catcalling in anticipation of Loretta's attentions. Someone squawks like a parrot. And before the CNA can make it to the bathroom door, Bleak's host voids its bladder.

"Kenny!" Loretta gasps. "This is a brand new uniform. Ooohh, I could just shake you!"

As Loretta carries him into the bathroom, the Stalker of Men sighs.

Nightfall is still a long way off.

***

When it comes, Bleak closes the host's eyes. Beyond that and the ability to soil himself, he doesn't have many options. Closing his eyes sharpens his concentration when the Night Mother appears.

She comes, shimmering like a black diamond; many faceted Atropos, mighty Ereshkigal, Oya, Yoruban avatar of the primal flame; yet none of these. She holds an ancient terror in Her gaze; the power to scourge him with his worst fears burns in Her face. Bleak averts his mind's eye.

He has sat beneath Her table far too long; since the August night in 1922, the night when Reverend Rufus Bleak fell, as they say Lucifer Morningstar fell.

Bleak and Dewey, his most trusted deacon, had taken up with two union men, Northerners, hoping to rouse the local cotton workers to protest the conditions in old Bull Emory's fields.

They were on their way to a rally when seven hooded white men in a black Ford ran them off the road. The men dragged Bleak, his wife Marie and three others from Dewey's old Edsel. They beat Brother Washington to death, stove in the side of his head like a hot loaf of bread and spilled his brains all over that dark country road. The Kluxers grabbed little Jimmy Payson and held him down while they beat Bleak and the others.

"You go tell the nigger lovers and union organizers at that church that they ain't welcome down here, boy."

Then the men raped Bleak's wife.

"Drag her over here! Get her down...down in the dirt!"

Afterward, they shot the organizers, leaving the nigger preacher to linger with a bullet burning in his guts.

But Bleak didn't cross over.

Because She was there, shining at the boundary of what Bleak would later come to think of as his old life. She was there. And She held salvation in Her hundred hands.

"Just as I am here now."

The Night Mother rears up, hive-queen, black as midnight, deadly as a dying man's dream. Bleak burns, fired in the crucible of Her dreadful radiance. He is a dead thing – yes - but he is also the memory of a living man and Her power is agony.

The Night Mother passes a shrieking fragment of that power into Bleak. In response, he rises from his host.

Bodiless, Bleak hovers. Over in one corner, an orderly is watching the small television mounted in the wall above the bathroom door.

"That's the news for this bright and sunny morning, the first day of January 2022. Have a safe and Happy New Year everyone."

One hundred years, Bleak thinks.

Then he fades.

***

When he opens his eyes he is standing in an alley. He's in a city, a northern city from the looks of it. The body She has made for him is strong. Bleak can feel muscles like steel rods beneath supple skin.

Bleak looks to his left. A darkened warehouse looms high overhead. He moves, lightning quick into the shadows between the buildings. He inhales; pauses...

And drives his right fist into the wall. The impact smashes brick to powder. When he steps back, the skin of his hand is unmarked.

Bleak whistles softly.

Then he steps into the alley and starts walking. He chooses no particular direction. His steps are guided by a Power far greater than himself. His faith enfolds him as deeply as the shadows She commands. The blessed assurance that once eluded him, embraces him now.

It's a modern city. That much he can tell. Bleak tastes the energies generated by millions of electrical devices around him. Luminous advertisements touting soft drinks or holographic entertainments adorn the night sky. Spotlights play among super skyscrapers. The air is foul. Bitter pollutants singe the lining of his nostrils. Overhead, a well lit, private transport drifts toward the HOLLYWOOD sign nestled in the hills.

Bleak nears a dark intersection; a black sedan cruises by on his left. The driver is concealed behind tinted glass. It's a well maintained Oldsmobile, gasoline powered but free of excessive exhaust.

There you are, Bleak thinks.

The Prize.

The Oldsmobile slides into the east, toward the barrios of East LA. Bleak steps into the street and follows. He keeps to the shadows, hidden from his prey. Up ahead, the Oldsmobile takes a sudden turn and veers off onto a side street, moving into the hills. Bleak follows; flitting between pools of light cast by intelligent streetlamps.

Beneath the eye of one of those streetlamps, three masked men rifle a dead man's pockets. The murderers freeze as a black wind howls past. When it has gone, they return to their work. Later, the men will murder each other, their minds consumed by their darkest fears.

Bleak shadows the Oldsmobile until a flash of brake light warns him. The car rolls to a halt in front of a chain link fence between two abandoned houses.

The driver climbs out and runs to the fence. He stops. Turns. His eyes flicker toward the place where Bleak hovers; figment of a dark dreamer.

Bleak watches the man's hands flutter in and out of his pockets. The driver walks with a pronounced limp.

Nodding to himself, the driver reaches up and bends a section of the fence back and down, forming a makeshift opening. Then he scuttles back to the Oldsmobile, climbs behind the wheel and closes the door.

The black sedan rolls through the opening in the fence and stops. The driver gets out, closes the opening behind him and hurries back. The Oldsmobile rolls down an embankment and out of sight.

Bleak glides across the street.

The embankment leads to a narrow, concrete roadway which winds down and around a corner, probably an access into the reservoir system that honeycombs this part of Southern California. The red glow from the sedan's taillights has almost faded when Bleak flows up and over the fence. He follows the light down into the darkness.

The night sounds of the city echo along the river basin walls and grow dim, then distant. The lights of the business district recede into the west. The driver navigates the dry riverbed. He never veers. *He'll choose a place where he feels secure,* Bleak thinks. *Where no one will hear the screams.*

The Oldsmobile stops beneath an overpass. Bleak melds into the shadows. The driver cuts the engine but leaves the headlights on.

He'll need light to work by, Bleak thinks.

The driver gets out of the sedan and opens the trunk. He whistles as he works. Bleak can hear him muttering to himself.

"...didn't think you'd come, but you did. Told you I had the juice, but you wouldn't listen."

As Bleak draws near, the driver produces a battered, red toolbox. He rattles it, like a child trying to guess the contents of his first present on Christmas morning.

"Merry Christmas, Daddy," a voice whispers.

Bleak spins, his fist cocked...

But he is alone in the darkness.

"Rufus, the boy's too young."

"Every boy needs a huntin' rifle, Marie..."

Bleak snarls at his ghosts until they fade.

"Gonna see what makes her run, son," the driver chuckles. "Gonna take her apart and see what's shakin'."

The driver walks around to the front of the Oldsmobile and sets the toolbox down on the hood. He takes a picnic basket and blanket off the back seat. Still humming, he spreads the blanket out on the concrete and opens the toolbox. Bleak sees moonlight dancing along the edge of a bright steel blade.

The driver opens the basket; removes something that looks like a silver platter and sets it on the blanket.

"Little picnic," he says. "Then we'll see."

Despite himself, Bleak holds his breath. He knows without question; he has found the Mother's choice. Bleak stills his mind and calls upon his faith, so unlike that which abandoned him long ago.

The driver stands and moves around to the Oldsmobile's passenger door. He opens the door and stoops down to peer inside.

"Get out."

A woman's hand reaches out of the darkness of the Oldsmobile. The nails gleam in the car light, so red they look black.

The driver snorts. Then he giggles.

125

"You gotta be kiddin' me, lady," the driver says. Nevertheless, he performs a mock bow, takes his passenger's hand and helps her out of the car. They stand that way for a moment, limned in starlight, her hand in his, a grim pas de deux, this silent ballet.

The woman is tall.

She wears an evening gown - black - with high heels to match. Her skin is pale. Her features resemble the aquiline cast adored by European nobility. Her neck supports a face all sharp angles and flat planes; full lips, high forehead beneath light brown hair she has been pacified, pulled up behind her head and tethered with something that sparkles. In the moonlight, the tall woman looks like an empress.

The driver is dark - his ethnicity uncertain - Latin or Greek. His eyes devour the tall woman. Then he spits in her face.

"I'm going to gut you like a dirty white fish," the driver says.

The Empress nods, seemingly at peace with this news.

"You'd like that, wouldn't you?" he says.

The Empress reaches out, her hands tracing gently the driver's brow and cheek, the contour of his jaw. The driver shudders. Then he grips her wrists, yanks her hands away from his face.

"Whore."

The Empress laughs; his spittle cooling on her cheek.

Bleak drifts closer, enough to see a rivulet of blood trickle from her nose. The driver's back is to him. Bleak could take him now, but he needs to understand.

Why doesn't she scream?

He sees the emptiness in her eyes, the way she caresses her abuser's cheek, and he knows. The driver is one of them. A Carrier. He has compelled the Empress, probably with no more effort than his focused will. He has used his disease to lure her to her own butchering.

Just like Reggie Whitehead, Bleak thinks.

Whitehead was a defiler and murderer of children. He'd slaughtered a dozen innocents by the time Bleak caught up with him outside Tallahassee.

Whitehead was a Carrier, one of the creatures the newspapers were calling *Magin.* Many believed that the *Magin* were harbingers of the End Times, soldiers in a conflict between Good and Evil that would either redeem humanity or destroy it. Others held that they were simply mankind's planetary replacements as Cro-Magnon replaced Neanderthal.

Whitehead too, had possessed the ability to fool the senses. With Bleak's hands wrapped around his throat, Whitehead assumed the form of old Dewey Washington.

"Brother Washington and I built this place with our bare hands."

"Preach, Reverend!"

Bleak banishes his memories.

The driver tests the edge of his cutting implement against his thumb; sucks the blood.

"Come here," he says.

The Empress shudders. Her head shakes back and forth. Bleak hears a whine building in the back of her throat.

"No..." she says.

The driver's eyes narrow to slits. Somewhere from the west, a train whistle pierces the silence. The driver turns his head *toward* the sound. Bleak senses the tension in the air ease. The Empress blinks once. Twice. She takes a step backward, as if staggered by a sudden wind.

"What...? What's happening?" she says. The Empress's eyes, alert now, dart back and forth.

"What's happening?"

Then her gaze locks on the driver. He stands silhouetted in the glare of the Oldsmobile's headlights.

"Who is that? Who's there?"

Exposed, the driver pauses. He shakes his head; clears his throat.

"Come here," he says.

But his voice is less certain.

The Empress shakes her head, backs out of the glare. Bleak senses the tension shift between them; two souls twisting in an undertow. His connection to the Mother has made him sensitive to the presence of the unseen.

"Come...come back," the driver says.

He steps toward the Empress and stumbles; his infirmity now more pronounced. The Empress's eyes widen.

"Nick? Nick Santos?"

"I SAID COME HERE!"

The driver lunges for the tall woman. And in that moment, she bolts.

Her name is Helen Mathison and she has existed in a waking nightmare for the last three hours. Awake, she remembers the truth of this man, and the red rage in him. She has bathed in the stinking abattoir behind his eyes. Even now, his power is a stabbing shriek in her mind.

Fear pushes her screaming out into the night.

But the driver's fingers clutch at flying strands of her hair. He snags a handful of her, pulls her down. With one blow he stretches her out on the concrete. Her head strikes the ground and she lies still.

The driver bends to tear at her as he has done in his dreams for the last six weeks. Tonight he will ease the fury that eats at him when they pass each other every day, in the halls of her beautiful museum. He will show the Great Lady that he is more than just a mop with a Mexican attached to it.

But a piece of the starless sky rears up behind him. The shadow - less an absence of light than its renunciation - whirls with power, a storm of lethal darkness. The driver screams. And the shadow falls. Unprepared, he staggers; smothered, pummeled by hammer blows that would kill an ordinary man.

The driver is no ordinary man.

He cannot step proudly into the spotlight that follows the other *magin*. He knows what the spotlight will reveal should it train its glow on him, and so he has kept his awesome secret all to himself.

But he has put the secret to good use. He has murdered thirty-two women across five states. He has left a swath of death in his wake like few others in the secret history of this bright new underworld.

But Rufus Bleak has left a wider swath.

The driver raises his fists, and the fire that consumed his sanity burns away the living shadows that surround Bleak. His talent blunts the force of Bleak's attack. Undaunted, Bleak steps back and leaps high over the driver's head, aiming a kick intended to break the man's neck.

The driver is agile despite his infirmity. He pivots and swings a booted foot into the center of Bleak's back; slams him into the basin wall. Bleak flows out of the way as the driver scores the side of the basin with the hunting knife. The driver turns, too fast, and assumes a defensive stance.

Bleak attacks; his fist passes through the space the driver's head occupied a moment earlier. The driver counters left, then loops his right fist toward Bleak's temple. The Stalker ghosts backward, evading the blow. The silver snarl of light from the driver's left fist slashes through the bridge of his nose and tears the flesh from his right cheek. Pain, immediate and surprising, crackles across the nerve endings in Bleak's face. He pauses, confused, and the driver slashes a burning trench across his chest.

Focus, man.

Bleak pushes the pain away. There is no pain when he serves Her truly.

But the driver's talent involves perception. With each attack, he drives his will against Bleak's mind. Grinning, the driver cuts the fingers from Bleak's left hand. His rage is a silent detonation. Blades of malice and memory flay Bleak's subtle flesh.

Nigger lovers...

Bleak staggers. The driver's disease delves deeper, searching until it finds the thing it seeks - the best place from which to strike - the long lost life of Rufus Bleak.

"...unionist sons o' bitches they ain't welcome in Carlton County..."

A cut to the jaw.

"Get her down in the dirt so the preacher can see..."

A backhanded slash mangles Bleak's throat.

"Look at her squirm, boys! I believe she likes it after all!"

A slicing blow to the chin snaps his neck.

"Sister, where's Marie? Where's my wife?"

"Hush, Rufus. She's in God's hands now."

Then all worlds end in thunder and blood.

Something moving; shining in the void. A force as cold as the heart of Death listens. It offers damnation, salvation, for a dead man's prayer.

"She screamed while they - took turns - with her. They ground her face into the dirt. They killed my whole congregation. Father God, I ask for justice."

"*No,*" the cold thing breathes. "*Not the father. The Mother of Night. Serve me and you will live, for as long as the darkness lasts.*"

"You would redeem my life?"

"*Yes.*"

"What do you ask in return?"

"*Only that you prepare the Way.*"

***

The driver rises, eyes shining and flat as a Mississippi cottonmouth's. Confident, renewed by bloodshed, his will is strong. The Empress stands, walks to him and, dreaming, bares her throat to his blade.

And Rufus Bleak chooses once more.

Power pushes him back up into the living world. He rises - his body a ruined hulk. The driver turns, realizing his danger too late.

Bleak screams.

His shout rips away the veil between past and present, life and death; his pain a serenade of atrocity that pierces flesh and penetrates bone.

The driver straightens, pinioned by power - his eyes widening. His mind ignites and burns like dry kindling.

"My...God," he whispers.

131

The effort costs him in flesh as he bites through his tongue. Blood fills his mouth; paints his chin.

"Pleeease," he whispers. "It hurts."

Bleak howls again.

The driver's brain, once a safe harbor for the disease, spills its secrets across the dry riverbed. The corpse remains standing, as if supported by a remnant of the driver's former power even in death. Headless, it falls.

Bleak feels nothing. The driver's ultimate fate is beyond his wisdom or care. He is a dead thing, inured to the weariness of a body, exhausted nonetheless.

"Happy New Year, Rufe."

This time, he doesn't bother to chase away the voices. He is tired, and memories are all he has left.

A gentle touch falls on Bleak's shoulder.

"Are you alright?"

The Empress.

Bleak hears the fear in her. They have shared a kind of Communion tonight. She has borne witness and has been changed, as he was changed.

'In the blinking of an eye,' he thinks.

Bleak looks to the light in the eastern sky; he crouches. Better to conceal himself from her; the extent of his injuries.

"I am," he says, simply. "Your name?"

"Helen," the Empress replies. "Helen Mathison. You're hurt. Let me help you."

For the first time in a century, Rufus Bleak smiles. It is a bitter smile, filled with a longing that can never be slaked. He smiles...and he strikes.

The Empress dies unaware of Bleak's betrayal. He catches her as she falls; gathers her in his arms and for a moment -

Marie
- his wife peers out at him from the eyes of Helen Mathison.

This woman, so different...

Yet somehow, they are the same.

She is tonight's Prize, a pawn in a game too vast for Rufus Bleak to understand.

Her will be done, he thinks. But he is uncertain now. He is empty when he slumps down next to her body. Miles distant, his host, a dying man named Kenny Cortez, gasps. Then the chord that binds them frays and snaps.

When the sun rises, there will be a new host, another Prize. Until then, Bleak will return to the void to await Her pleasure. The Mother is nothing if not pragmatic.

Dying again, the Stalker of Men thinks of the night he exacted his revenge on the men who murdered his belief, their screams when they finally knew him for what he was. They called out to their god and were forsaken, as he was forsaken.

This time, the smell of pine brings him back.

As sunlight pries his eyelids apart, Bleak remembers the inconstancy of gods: Powers at play in a shifting sea of mortal yearning.

Then he makes his choice.

One hundred years, he thinks. Long enough.

His refusal will mean the real death. The Mother demands no less. But he has sacrificed too many souls to sate her dark appetites. Tonight, he will offer his own as a measure of recompense for the lives he has destroyed in her name.

The thought of his ending warms him; he has not been warm in nearly a century. He will serve no messiahs.

Salvation and damnation, he thinks. *Same coin, different sides.*

But as the sun crawls across the sky, Bleak prays for the strength to reject the gods he cannot change.

THE LAST AMERICAN PRESIDENT

Dear Dairy,

Today in the Oval Office, the Secretary of Defense tried to swallow his own intestines. It was hard work. They were slippery. The slimy suckers just kept gushing out of Secretary Halvorsen's mouth and wrapping themselves around my National Security Advisor's throat like wet red boa constrictors.

Hally kept making these awful retching sounds. He begged and bounced and hollered like a man cho-hoodlin' down the crapper while trying not to shit himself. No doubt about it, Diarie: whatever the Vox Mortis had slipped into him wanted out in the worst kind of way.

Halvorsen shot up out of his chair (to gain more leverage on those guts I imagine) and accidentally elbowed the British Prime Minister in the nose. Prime Minister Bell back flipped out of his chair and slid under the War Table. It was a good thing too, because it was right about then that the Pope turned into a saber toothed tiger and bit Joan Collins's left arm off.

While the Papal saber tooth was looking for a place to eat Vice President Collins, Gene Palmer, my National Security Advisor turned blue and expired; throttled by the Secretary of Defense's chittlin's.

Outside, Hell was bending civilization over a log and making it squeal like a Christmas pig.

Something big, like Godzilla big, strode past the barricaded windows that overlooked Constitution Avenue. I think it was the Leader of the Vox, the one whose name (if spoken aloud) has the power to transmute your bones into ground glass.

Over across the mall, a female Vox was performing an act of double penetration on the Washington Monument. Christian decency forbids my describing it, Diarie. Let's just say that Congress outlawed such acts back in '02, except for those constrained by the bonds of holy heterosexual wedlock as defined by our Lord and Savior Jesus Christ Himself. Hell, we're gonna need the entire National Guard just to douche that sucker off.

As Hally's other organs began to chew their way out through his asshole, the Dalai Lama Number Who Gives A Rat's Ass got up and tried to help. He pushed his glasses up on his nose and grasped the spitting entrails that were boiling out of Halvorsen's mouth. But before the D.L. could offer anything more than an earnest tug, Vice President Collins reared up from behind the Dirty Harry pinball machine. The Papal saber tooth hadn't left much of her: only an arm, her torso, most of her legs and half of her face remained, but the people of the U.S.A hadn't chosen J.C. as their V.P. for n-o-t-h...n-u-t-h...

Aw Hell, Dairy, I don't have to spell it out for you.

With the same pluck she'd displayed during her wonderful acting career, the Vice President dragged herself across the room and tore the Dalai Lama's face off. The fact that J.C. was over eighty years old didn't slow her down. The fact that she was dead didn't stop her from ripping that peace-loving pacifist a new asshole. Literally.

Oh well, good riddance to bad rubbish I say. The D.L. was the biggest pain in the ass to my administration; always going on about "peace" and "compassion" and "democracy" and blah blah blah blah blah.

Speaking of pains in the ass, I can't believe what the female Vox did with the Monument after she'd pleasured herself. Christian decency forbids me to describe it, Dairy. Let's just say that when we made partial birth abortions in the United States punishable by death, we should have included "Extra-dimensional Iterations of the United States" as well. As of this writing, there's a smoking fifty foot long Vox fetus skewered atop the monument. It's just hanging there squirming like a titanic black maggot.

Occasionally, the fetus extrudes its tentacles down to the ground to snatch up a mess of unwary soldiers and cram them into one of the terrible gaping maws that pucker what I'm taking to be its ass end. (I call it the ass-end because of the river of crap that comes pouring out of it every thirty seconds, enough to cover the monument with the foulest smelling matter I've seen since we started drilling the Labrea Tar Pits.)

Dr. Maisiella Fletchet, my Secretary of State, pulled her head out from under my desk and whipped a nine millimeter .357 Desert Eagle automatic out of the thigh holster she wore attached to her black leather corset.

As the dead Vice President sprang toward me, the Secretary of State opened up on her with that big black beautiful piece of hardware (the gun, not Maisy). What was left of the V.P. splattered like the Blue Ribbon Squealer at the NASCAR ANNUAL HOG STOMP (At which, incidentally, I had the great honor of throwing out last year's Black Piglet.)

Funny, I never thought about it, Diarie, but it seems like that was just about when the Troubles began.

That's when the Vox Mortis invaded Earth.

The Leader of the Vox, the one with the lethal name, was the first to step out of the great rip in space/time that appeared over Washington. He was the one who first informed the media about his damned race of devils, demons, witches and whores.

They'd crossed over from another reality, he claimed, "from an Earth eons in advance of this one. One which cast the original cosmic shadow that spawned this pallid reflection."

Yeah. Sure.

They call themselves the Vox Mortis, the Voice of Death; a race of pirates, murderers, and parasites who travel time and space feasting on the physical agonies and psychic misery of so-called "lesser" Earths, depleting their resources, enslaving billions of intelligent beings to help expand their "Vast Empire."

A vast empire? Interdimensional travel by alien giants who stalk the spaceways torturing innocent people, impregnating unwilling women, eating children and butt fucking Mother Nature 'til she rolls over and craps pink lemonade?

What kind of idiot do the Vox take me for?

I'll tell you what they really are, Diury.

Demons. Hellspawn. Evil.

I'm talking Big Technicolor Evil with digital sound, Evil on the half-shell; Evil that could only be foisted on the world by that red-faced trickster who fell from our Creator's Loving Grace a couple thousand years ago solely to cause wholesale planetary chaos.

That's right, Dairy: I'm talking about Ted Kennedy.

Just kiddin.' I had him executed years ago.

It's the End Times alright. I just happen to be the one whom the Lord hath chosen to witness His Final Judgment.

"Die, you incense sniffing motherfucker!" Maisy screamed. Then she blew the saber-toothed Pope's brains out. Maisy was a lapsed Catholic herself. Maybe that's why she was smiling when she pulled the trigger.

Maisy did a victory dance atop the Popecat's corpse, the barricades dropped off the doors. Then the doors swung open and a big red Indian walked into the room.

The Indian was wearing full ceremonial headdress, buckskins and moccasins, and leading a dinosaur on a leash.

The dinosaur was muzzled. The "Native American" (Hell, I still think of them as redskins even *after* what happened when the Vox stole Boston and replaced it with a city-sized open air cannibal market) was not.

The Indian looked a lot healthier than most folks, seeing as how we'd outlawed exercise back in '01. I mean by 1989 the air and water were so bad that anyone without nose, lung and rectal filters stood about as much chance of escaping a life threatening disease as a crack whore working an AIDS camp at Chernobyl.

Hell, I wondered. How'd we miss him?

The dinosaur wasn't big. It stood only about eight foot high. It was smooth, not scaly like the carnosaurs the Vox sicced on Texas when they first invaded. It sported a long, waving tail and a friendly, open expression. If it wasn't for all the blood and bits of rotted flesh encrusted on its jaws I might have sworn it was smiling at me.

Oh, and it was purple.

"Freeze, scumbag," Maisy snarled, her Desert Eagle leveled and ready. The big Indian looked at the two of us for a moment. Then he spoke.

"I'm called Tom Hawk," he said. "I'm here to turn out the lights."

Maisy squinted and cocked her head like she hadn't heard him right.

"What did you just say?" she said.

The purple dinosaur growled, a deep rumble that rolled up from its belly. Tom Hawk soothed it with some soft words and a snatch of song. For a moment, I thought I smelled wildflowers on the burning wind, a shimmer of Spring that danced across the War Table and prickled my nostrils.

I sneezed. My son-of-a-bitchin' allergies were playing up on me again.

The smell only lasted for a moment. Soon enough the tang of incipient sunshine was replaced by the odor of frying flesh wafting in off the Potomac.

"I said I'm here to turn out the lights, sweetheart," Hawk said. "You assholes are done."

Maisy lifted one bushy eyebrow and hissed, "Terrorist."

"Uh oh," I said.

Whatever was about to go down, it was gonna go down ugly. Maisy had a hard-on for towel-head reprobates, even though we'd never actually met one, and with his crazy, ethnic get-up and earthen pot complexion, Hawk looked enough like a Muslim fundamentalist to merit a high velocity Teflon jacketed Come-to-Jesus.

Maisy lifted the Desert Eagle and pulled the trigger a nanosecond before Prime Minister Bell popped up from behind the War Table. Bell never saw it coming. A fist- sized chunk of the PM's skull flew across the room and knocked my Ronald Reagan commemorative bust off its solid gold pedestal.

Maisy snarled and squeezed off another shot. The reinforced walls of the Oval Office rang as the cop killer slug struck the barricade directly behind Tom Hawk. I ducked as it spanged off the brass menorah I was using as a toast rack. Maisy screamed, clutched her throat and dropped to the floor.

"Maisy!" I screamed. I fell to my knees and scooped her up in my arms. Blood was everywhere. "Goddamit!"

I'd already lost my parents, most of my friends and my in-laws to the invasion. My wife Lonnie - only three days in her grave - had been torn apart and eaten by something that looked like a giant carnivorous hemorrhoid. I wasn't about to lose the best piece of tail I'd ever had to boot.

"Love you, pookie," Maisy rasped as black blood bubbled up from between her luscious lips. "I'm...I'm..."

"Shhhh," I shushed. "You're gonna be alright."

The wound to her throat looked bad, but not mortal. I thought she stood a decent chance if I could get her to one of those emergency trauma centers.

Then Hawk freed the purple dinosaur.

The creature leapt up onto my War Table, iron talons gouging white tracks into its imported mahogany goodness. Then it shrieked like one of Satan's harlots and sprang toward us.

I hauled my white ass outta there.

The purple dinosaur landed claws first on Maisy and began to stomp. As my honey pop screamed, the dinosaur bit and tore at her with those terrible flesh-clogged choppers. It gutted her the way

I gutted Social Security back in '06. That goddamned thing did the Camel Walk all over my little chocolate bunny until there was nothing left but red sludge.

I snatched up Maisy's automatic, pointed it at the dinosaur and fired five shots into its purple skull. The monster's head exploded. Then it fell face first into the mess it had made of my sweet black hoochie mama.

I spun and leveled the Desert Eagle at the redskin.

"You ain't getting' me, Chief," I snarled. I had three bullets left and I wasn't aiming to waste 'em.

"I didn't come for you, dickhead," Hawk shot back. "I came to turn out the lights. You get to watch."

"Oh yeah?" I said. "Watch this, Mahatma."

God Laughs When You Die

I pulled the trigger three times. Maisy's gun made the Big Bang Bang and the Indian fell over like a dead redwood. I let out a rebel yell and ran over to kick the corpse.

Hawk opened his eyes, sat up and spat out the three slugs. Then he grabbed me and dragged me toward the barricaded picture window.

"Wait!" I said. "Now you just wait one goddamn minute!"

Hawk rammed my head and shoulders through the thin wooden slats, breaking the window glass. Ice and ash filled up my lungs. It was the first time I'd breathed air outside the Office since the Ebola Wars destroyed Philadelphia. I gagged on a stench reminiscent of rotten eggs, burning flesh and human waste.

Across the way, the Leader was painting the white dome of the Jefferson Memorial using an emptied-out tour bus filled with human entrails.

Dairy, I consider myself a tough man, a cowboy: rough and ready for terrorists, civil unrest, Affirmative Action or any other evil that might arise. But when I saw the image the Leader had slathered across the Memorial I felt my courage take off and skip naked across the Rose Garden of my mind.

The Indian whistled a piercing blast that ruptured my right eardrum and the Leader of the Vox turned toward us. He smiled, his perfect teeth shining like a blaze of lightning, and gave Hawk a "thumbs-up."

The Indian didn't let me savor that vision of Hell for long before he jerked me back inside. Then he punched me in the chest. I felt three ribs crack like wet twigs. While I gasped on the floor of the Oval Office, Hawk made me watch while he took a fire axe to my War Table.

143

"No!" I wheezed. I'd scored more tail on that table than Oprah Winfrey'd had hot dinners, but when Hawk was done there wasn't nothing left but a ten thousand dollar pile of firewood.

"Time to go, pookie," he said. "Take off your clothes."

The last thing he did was turn out the lights.
Then he threw me out of the Oval Office.

As I lay there butt naked on the sidewalk with the world burning down around me, Hawk grabbed me by the hair, pulled me to my feet and whispered one word into my ear.

"Run."

I ran.

Now, I sit here, Dairy, hiding inside this burnt-out old bus station wearing a dead man's clothes, while the demons hunt me down. One of 'em almost got me the other day, a big black bastard of a thing that walked like a man and looked like a killer whale with a mouthful of steel teeth. I had to hide in the sewers to escape the fucker.

I couldn't hide down there for long, however. The Dead have taken over the sewers and they have an uncanny knack for tracking warm meat.

I found the bus station this morning.

It was filled with regular dead people - folks slaughtered trying to get out of the city. I could have told them, Dairy. No place is safe. Before the satellites and radio went offline I watched the Vox striding like God's Justice through every major city on Earth, entire legions of the Damned shuffling in their wake. It's only a matter of time before they smoke me out.

The Leader of the Vox has set a bounty on me, you see?

"The human who brings me the head of the American President will earn power; territories vast and yielding to his every dark desire."

See, I'm the reason they're here, Dairy.

The Vox were drawn by the anguish my friends and I "inflicted" upon humanity, or so they claim. Now the whole world wants to hack my head off in the worst frigging way.

I've secured myself a spot in the janitor's closet, all boarded up and locked in tight, but it's only a temporary solution. Five minutes ago, the corpses in the bus station stood up and started screaming. I can hear them hunting for me even as I write these words.

But I've got a crazy idea.

I'm thinking if I play it right, maybe somebody with friends in Low places will hook me up. Maybe somebody'll give me a job. Who knows? If I'm smart, I might just pull off the biggest comeback since Hitler invaded Manhattan. I've got the experience. *Hell, the Vox already admire my work.* And I think I can teach the Leader a thing or two about human suffering.

The screamers are right outside my closet now, Dairy. They're ripping down the barricades. It's showtime.

I'm ready, you fuckers.

Bring it on.

Michael Boatman

By day, Michael Boatman is also an actor. For six seasons he played "Carter" on the ABC comedy Spin City (for which he was nominated for three NAACP Image Awards for Best Supporting Actor in a Comedy Series). For seven seasons he played 'Stanley' on the HBO series Arli$$. (Four Image Award nominations). Other notable television performances include 'Beckett', in the Vietnam drama China Beach, and 'Attorney Dave Seaver' on NBC's Law and Order and Law and Order S.V.U. He appears in the feature films, Woman Thou Art Loosed, The Glass Shield, The Peacemaker, Hamburger Hill and many others. In 2003, he co-starred in the Broadway production of Athol Fugard's drama, Master Harold...and the boys.

His short stories and novellas appear in Weird Tales (Oct 2007); Lords of Justice (Carnifexpress. 2007); Until Someone Loses An Eye...Tales of Disturbing Humor (Bradford House/Twisted Publishing); BADASS HORROR (Dybbuk Press); Dark Dreams II: Voices From The Other Side, and Dark Dreams III: Whispers in The Night (Kensington Books). He is the author of the horror comedy novel The Revenant Road. (Drollerie Press. 2008). His horror- comedy film, Evil Woman, is scheduled to begin pre-production in Fall of 2007, (Guardian Entertainment).

He lives in New York with his wife, Myrna and their four children.

2

Printed in the United States
204185BV00003B/1-30/A